From DAWN to DUSK

God Bless All you Do!

Jim Hunt

JIM HUNT

All Scripture is from the *New International Version of the Holy Bible* (Zondervan Bible Publishers, Grand Rapids, MI, 1978), unless otherwise noted.

Cover illustration by Zachary Hunt

Copy editing by Dan Shenk of CopyProof, Goshen, IN

Layout by Sties Design Agency, LLC, Goshen, IN

Printed by Evangel Press, Nappanee, IN

ISBN-13: 978-0-9886711-0-2

Printed in the United States of America

Dedication

This book is dedicated to my father, James Austin Hunt, for whom I have tremendous respect, and who has been my mentor throughout my life, even though he died in 1955 when I was 16 years of age. I must add that my brothers and sisters have been my teachers and best friends.

Contents

Author's Preamble

When considering whom to ask to write the Foreword for this book, only my three brothers came to mind. Our lives are so intertwined through my 73 years that there is no one who knows me better than these guys. Several memories:

- We built forts together as children and put together our own pole-vaulting equipment, with a real sand pit. For our standards we used 2×4's with nails. The crossbar was bamboo, and we used bamboo for the vaulting pole. (You certainly wanted to stay in the middle so you didn't hit the nails.)
- We sold milk bottles and soft drink bottles picked up at new home construction sites: 3 cents for the milk bottle and 2 cents for the soft drink bottle.
- We swam in creeks and in the flooded basements of those construction sites.

- We fished together and ice skated (until we were frozen ourselves) on the lake near our home.
- We rode miles on our bikes together to buy penny bubble gum after World War II.
- We teamed up together to beat the socks off anyone in the neighborhood who would take us on in football, basketball, or baseball.
- We ran a restaurant in the '50s when the oldest brother (Don) was 21 and the youngest (Charlie) was just 11.
- In the '60s we developed a wholesale pizza business called Pepe's Pizza, which expanded into 20 states.
- In 1990 my brothers and I started an all-new company called Hunt Brothers Pizza, which is now in 28 states.

While the four of us are grateful for our success, I would be out of line if I didn't thank and compliment all the awesome people who have influenced us and who today make up Hunt Brothers Pizza.

Over the years Don, Lonnie, Charlie, and I have held each other accountable on many occasions. This book is directed toward my children and grandchildren in the hope that they will understand the importance of brotherly love and sticking together, that by working together they will be stronger than working by themselves, and that there's no one better to "have your back" than a brother.

—Jim Hunt, Author
Co-Founder of Hunt Brothers Pizza

Foreword

Very seldom does a person of uncommon intelligence produce a manuscript that has the unique ability to not only reorganize thought patterns but also literally motivate changes in thoughts, words, actions, and how one's life is lived.

As you read and reread this book, you will find exquisite literary gems hidden within my brother's descriptions of his successes and failures, joys and disappointments. These pearls of wisdom will offer hope, encouragement, vision, and direction to anyone who truly seeks "LIFE," instead of "just living."

—Don Hunt
Business partner for more than 50 years and brother for 73 years; Co-Founder of Hunt Brothers Pizza

As an older brother of Jim Hunt, I have known him from the time he was a toddler ... sitting in the driveway picking up rocks to admire the bugs underneath.

This younger brother grew and developed to become a father of eight beautiful children and respected owner of a multi-million-dollar company.

The years in between were sometimes heaven and sometimes hell. Through it all, Jim has made some great observations and gained some valuable insights. Most importantly, he has learned to approach the world with wonder and a positive attitude.

If a young man starts out thinking he will be a Catholic priest (quits that!), runs the family restaurant, joins the Marines, marries at age 30, has eight children while starting a tiny business that evolves into a national company ... this isn't luck! This is a man with convictions!

Jim's words of advice will "stick to your ribs" like Mother's Thanksgiving dinner, dessert and all.

—Lonnie J. Hunt
Brother and friend; Co-Founder of Hunt Brothers Pizza

If you have ever wished you had a mentor, a guide, or older person to give you some wisdom and some insight on how to succeed in business—or how to have a successful marriage or life—your wish may have just come true.

Jim Hunt, my brother, is a good friend as well. He's 73, and I'm 68, so I've known him long enough to form some opinions about his character.

Jim has been a close friend of God for a long time. And with that friendship has come wisdom. The Word of God states:

> *But the wisdom that comes from heaven is first of all pure; then peace loving, considerate, submissive, full of mercy and good fruit, impartial and sincere.*
>
> —James 3:17

Jim has received the wisdom that is from above. He is a living example of that wisdom in his everyday life—both personal and business. His humility, patience, kindness, and gentleness are evident to all who know him.

His generosity is a by-product of his faith in God's promises.

> *One man gives freely, yet gains even more;*
> *another withholds unduly, but comes to poverty.*

A generous man will prosper;
he who refreshes others will himself be refreshed.

—Proverbs 11:24–25

Jim isn't following rules so he can be loved by God. Instead, God's love conquered him. Jim saw God's love in His Son, Jesus.

For God so loved the world that he gave his one and only Son, that whoever believes in him shall not perish but have eternal life.

—John 3:16

As Jim has walked and talked with Jesus daily, he has became more like the Master over the course of his life. He has realized that God's love doesn't depend on his goodness but on God's goodness.

Jim has been a mentor to me, and I hope you will permit him to be a mentor you too.

A daily prayer by J. D. Greear has benefited me greatly; I hope it blesses you: "Dear Jesus, there is nothing I can do that would make You love me more, and nothing I have done that makes You love me less. Your presence and approval are all I need for everlasting joy. As You have been to me, so I will be to others. As I pray, I'll measure Your compassion by the cross and Your power by the Resurrection."

Thanks, Jim, for writing this book.

—Charles Hunt
Younger brother; Co-Founder of Hunt Brothers Pizza

Acknowledgments

As you will see, this book was started in 1973. It lay dormant for many years but now is finally completed nearly four decades later. I'm sure I needed time to season in my understanding of life.

First, I wish to thank my father, mother, brothers, sisters, and children, all of whom have influenced my entire life for the good.

Father Alban Berling of the Order of St. Benedict was my athletic coach and pastor; he taught me that I could step up to the plate and do more than I imagined. Sister Mary Matthew, also of the O.S.B., had the unique ability to inspire young boys and girls to be even more than they thought they could be.

I owe a debt of gratitude to James Allen who wrote *As a Man Thinketh,* which (by actual count) I've read 13 times since 1970.

Of all the books I've read, this one inspired me the most to write and gave me positive direction for my life.

The Word of God, the Bible, has been my guiding light through all the seasons of my life.

There are so many good people in the world who devote their lives to helping others. They have motivated me and others to also jump in and get involved in their mission. Below are only a few of the many who could be listed:

Titus Oyeyemi of African Projects for Peace and Love Initiatives, Mike Evans of the Jerusalem Prayer Team, Valerie Henderson of Lighthouse Ministries, Sandy and Jerry Tucker of Galilean Home Ministries, Larissa and Tom Benz of Bridges of Faith, Jim Connell of the Lexington Rescue Mission, Oral Roberts Ministries, and Kenneth Copeland Ministries.

Throughout my life I've studied and appreciated the teachings of the following men: Dale Carnegie, Napoleon Hill, Earl Nightingale, W. Clement Stone, Merlin Carothers, Sir John Templeton, John M. Cummuta, Paul J. Meyer, Norman Vincent Peale, and Ralph Waldo Emerson (as a boy I kept a 3×5 file of quotes, and Emerson's were my favorite).

I also want to thank Zig Ziglar who has been a vital influence in my life. He ingrained in me the belief that "you can have everything in life you want if you will just help enough other people get what they want."

Since this is the first book I've had published, I had no idea what all went into book production. I must acknowledge the many contributions of my editor, Dan Shenk, of CopyProof, Goshen, Indiana, who did so much more than edit this book. He could be listed as co-author! Thanks, Dan.

Another who "dares to be a Daniel" is Daniel Dean of Elkhart, Indiana, whose services CopyProof secured for the preliminary edit of this book. Because his many great suggestions almost made my head swim, his nickname could be Dizzy Dean.

Alison Sties of the Sties Design Agency, Goshen, worked minor miracles in designing the book and preparing it for Evangel Press, Nappanee, Indiana—all in time for Christmas 2012! She also selected most of the spot-on "pull quotes" sprinkled throughout the book.

My youngest son, Zachary Hunt, a budding artist and animator, lovingly rendered the cover drawing for this book.

Finally, I acknowledge the many contributions to this book project of my late wife, Cheryl, who trusted me and believed in me as long ago as 1974 when I said I wanted to take off a year to write. The literary seeds we planted together that year are now bearing fruit. I thank Cheryl and love her for her wonderful support over 38 years of marriage. And all glory to God for whatever harvest is reaped through the reading of this book.

James S. Hunt

To My Family

It is January 2011. The primary purpose of this writing is to communicate to our children and grandchildren the principles that Cheryl and I believe are most important for a productive, rewarding, and successful life. These are the things we have learned through trial and error. You will improve on these and find that some of our ideas don't work as well as some you discover. There are many ways to do a thing and attain good results. In this simple writing I share my thoughts in the hope that you will discover some diamonds within that will guide you on your journey through life. Each day is a new day that offers opportunity for your dreams to blossom into reality—and they will.

Cheryl and I have been so fortunate that our eight grown children are such wonderful people. This proves that love is the answer. We loved—and love—you dearly, and even though we made mistakes in raising you, we always showed love to you. When you give love, you receive love. *Love* is the key word.

But it wasn't always this way for me. Let's go back about four decades to some writing I did at that time.

– 1 –

Angry at 33

It is 1973. I am married to a beautiful, intelligent woman who loves me completely and whom I love. We have two healthy children. Yet I am disgusted, angry, fed up with what, it seems, life entails. I know that many thousands of other men and women all over the world feel the same as I do.

2011

Now in 2011, let me explain why I felt as I did in the summer of 1973. To do this I must give you my inner thoughts and some background. I will share so that together we may learn the way to prevent this ugly, festering, disgusting anger I was going through in hopes that you will never get to this place in your life. I was one of the men Thoreau wrote about in *Walden* who "lead lives of quiet desperation."

But, you see, there is a better way. With the economy as it is, morals as loose as they are, our governing people as they are, there is still a way to be happy, to have peace of mind and heart amid all the turmoil.

Come along with me to Peace of Mind. Again, I share with you some of my writings from nearly 40 years ago.

1973

The world is a dazzling spectrum of colors, beauty, sounds, pains, troubles, joys, fears, pleasures, opportunities, wants, desires, needs, likes, dislikes, successes, and failures. Man, it seems, strives to succeed. He is forced to compete, to want what he does not possess and to not appreciate what he does possess. Man is ever striving for more of the pleasures, more of the

> *We dream of more—more money, more fame, more success, more power, more sex.*

riches, that he hopes will make him more of a material success, an earthly success, in the eyes of his fellow strivers. To strive is to hope, and in hoping, we live our lives ever closer to our ultimate material, man-made object of hope, whatever it may be. We then have new hope, because once our human, earthly hopes are realized, we possess the object of that hope, and that material blob is then not as good as the proverbial green grass on the other side of the fence. We humans cannot appreciate life in its beautiful splendor; its magnificent pleasures are free, but nothing free is good enough. We dream of more—more money, more fame, more success, more power, more sex. More and more and more. We yearn for the best food, bigger homes, fancier automobiles, expensive clothes, and more and more and more.

So man lives his short span on this earth always striving for more, only to find that the more he gains, the poorer he becomes. The poorer because he must have more, and more is always an arm's length away. As infants we want everything and anything to stick in our mouths; this seems to carry on throughout our lives. Anything we possess, whether it be our fellow human in sex or a new automobile, is a pleasure only for a short time because we always have a new hope, a new desire to extinguish or satisfy; no thing is ever all we want. We strive and hope, hope to better ourselves financially. We go from one opportunity to another, never applying ourselves completely to any one opportunity because we are always looking for an easier and quicker way to succeed. We study and work and one day realize we are close to God's Judgment Day, our hopes are pipe dreams, and our days of life are spent. Are our values out of whack?

A boy has dreams of being a circus clown, a fireman, a policeman, a doctor, a writer, an artist, a lawyer, a dentist, a salesman. Or of being just like Dad. As a young man, he strives to be a millionaire, only to find it would be great simply to make ends meet, earn his living any way he can, and somehow get through old age to death with enough food and bedding one day at a time.

My thoughts are the thoughts of many men and women who think and look at what is and wonder, Why? They are the thoughts of many adult children not raised by their mothers and fathers because their parents were strivers, working for that next advertised blob of material junk that man says man must have to be successful, to really be happy.

My thoughts are the thoughts of many women and children who no longer have Father because he strived too hard, forced his human, God-given body to break, and died, leaving his family material junk that will rot with age. They wonder why they didn't slow him down and help him enjoy their love, enjoy their pleasures, and appreciate living instead of fighting to buy more.

2011

Time is all, time is everything, and time is the first cry of a newborn with healthy gums and no teeth to the last breath of a man with wrinkled, old gums and no teeth. Our time can be wonderfully used or foolishly wasted. God has given you and me a time to live on this earth. We must use our time well. Is striving for material things the best way to use our allotted time? I believe not! Man says yes, and the masses fall in line to follow. Our whole lives are spent trying to build ourselves up in the eyes of our fellow men. There must be a better way! Isn't there more to life than the day-in, day-out dollar earning? There must be more to life than this continual striving.

> *Our whole lives are spent trying to build ourselves up in the eyes of our fellow men. There must be a better way! ... There must be more to life than this continual striving.*

I became angry and disgusted with things the way I saw them.

I loved my father, and I admired and respected him, but he did not spend as much time with his family as we would have liked because he was the ultimate striver. He was a successful restaurant entrepreneur, and the restaurant business is not a 9-to-5 career. When I was with my father it was wonderful and was always a happy, conversational time. He showed his love for our mother and all of us. We seven children loved our parents and saw how much they loved each other. Dad lived through the Great Depression and knew the hardships of living without a proper income. I believe this background and a positive outlook on life were driving forces within him that made him a striver. He was respected by those for whom he had worked as a young man and for his wisdom as a businessman. Dad was a striver who died at a young age. He was a dedicated provider, and since he lived during the Depression he knew the value of a dollar. He pulled himself up by the bootstraps and was very successful. This was a man who was respected because of his integrity and because he strived daily to provide the best for his family. At the age of 46 he became eternally dependent on God because his heart stopped beating. Consequently he left his loving wife and seven children without a husband and father. This magnificent striver left us children many good traits. He taught us the reason for integrity, a good work ethic, and keeping our word, and he taught us to love, to think, to be ambitious, how to treat people, the importance of going to church as a family, and to strive to be the best at whatever we committed our minds or bodies to.

1973

As my thoughts proceed, I must inject here a very important one. I love many of the things money can buy, and I love work. I thank God for work; it is a blessing that we have work to do. Work has always been my hobby, as well as a source of financial income. But is there more to life than just working, marrying, raising children, and dying? You see, up to this point in my life I have always strived to better myself financially. Now, as I see gray hairs of age begin to show, I wonder about my goals. Sure, I have achieved some things that I am proud of, but what's it all about?

I sometimes wonder how it must have been as a farmer in a small town where life was slower and man appreciated God's gifts from His earth. There are times when I dream of living completely from nature, maybe on an island. Surviving on coconuts and berries and basking in the sun and the surf. I dream of being a child again and having a father to answer my call in need. But, unless there is a better way and I can be changed by it, I will continue to strive and work, hope and dream, be positive in my thoughts and actions because my fellow man respects that. When I am dead and lying there stiff as a board, will people say, "He was a good man, he was a striver, and now his wife is financially independent"? Will they say, "He was a great provider, and he sure was a worker"? Isn't there more to life than that?

A child is born, and the stay at the hospital is beautiful; it's a wonderful new world for the child. Everyone loves the new baby. He receives love; he's being breast-fed, and he's so happy. But then he is moved home with his parents who both work because they are strivers and want more of the material things, so the child is taken to a nursery and is fed a bottle. He is cared for by people who are not as caring as his parents and don't show the love he has become accustomed to. The child has stronger feelings toward the giants he's with at night than the ones who feed and care for him during the day, but he doesn't see much of his parents. His parents sleep at night, get him up early, and drop him off with other parents' screaming kids. This crazy situation goes on until the boy is old enough to go to preschool at 4 years of age! Then, through prekindergarten, kindergarten, and eight years of elementary school, the striving parents who fed, cared for, and loved the child as a newborn, but whom he now sees very little of, tell the child there is a Santa Claus, an Easter bunny, a God, a heaven, a hell, a Bible, a president of the United States, an America of the free and the brave. One day he finds out there is no Santa Claus; there is no Easter bunny; the existence of God, heaven, and hell are doubtful; the president might be tricky; and America may or may not be all it's cracked up to be. He begins to wonder about everything his parents say because they don't always go to church, and even if they do, churchgoing is the only sign of God or religion he ever sees or hears about at his home. America and her leaders are slandered on all sides by the media. The stories of Santa Claus and the Easter bunny are repeated so often that the child's discovery of the truth about these stories is a traumatic experience.

So, what's true, and what's a lie? Where's the line? Is there a God? Was Jesus just a good Jewish man whom many wrote stories about? Is the Bible just another story written to get us to conform to certain norms? Is America a country where good morals are not important, where marriage is no longer respected, and where too many of our governing people lack integrity? Is the family important for the proper growth of a child? Can a child believe what Mom and Dad tell him when his parents are part-time parents at best?

> *So, what's true, and what's a lie? Where's the line? Is there a God? Was Jesus just a good Jewish man whom many wrote stories about?*

A child born into this world is exposed to many different beliefs and standards. It's a world where right and wrong are learned through navigating many available beliefs, morals, and philosophies. A world where there are many different gods and religions, rules and standards that are hard to decipher. So the boy destined to become a man adopts man's ways and tries, strives, and hopes to climb the masses and have more material goods than the next man to prove his success.

– 2 –

Why I Had to Write About the Anger That Had Taken Over My Very Soul

1975

At 34 years of age last year, while employed by a very successful wholesale food company, holding the position of Executive Vice President, I wrote in searing anger and disgust the previous several pages. Financially, materially, everything was going in the right direction. We bought what we wanted when we wanted it, we dined at the finest restaurants, and our annual vacations to Florida were always in beautiful places.

By the age of 34, I had read every book I could get my hands on concerning the power of the mind and positive thinking. I believed I could do anything I set my mind to. All my faith was in No. 1—me. I started reading Edward Cayce's books, began studying hypnotism, and came very close to taking courses in extrasensory perception. I believed completely that mind control paved the way to ultimate success. Through mind control, I would achieve my material goals. I also believed that hard work, even at the sacrifice of a decent family life, was important if I wanted the riches of this world. Consequently, I traveled away from home on business so much that I wasn't able to enjoy my children's young years. (Watching our children grow and change each day is one of the greatest gifts God has given us.)

Traveling away from home five or six nights a week is not conducive to a moral or sober life. Certainly not all of us traveling away from our families succumb to immorality, but to those who do succumb I say there is a way to have the willpower to overcome the temptations encountered when traveling. It's a free gift that is available to all of us. Later, in another chapter, I will explain how you can receive this free gift that will change you forever. There are so many strivers in the world who are sacrificing their very souls in the name of financial success. Now, today, the temptations are at every turn

> *A number of times I thought if this is what it's going to be like until the day I die, I would be better off dead.*

in America. For the first five years of my married life, I traveled, and almost every night away I had some kind of alcoholic drink. Drinking helped me relax and sleep in the lonely hotels. A man who travels away from his family will at times have a heart-wrenching loneliness. This is a fact that thousands of really good men can attest to. The Lord never meant for man to travel away from his family without His help. A man had better have Jesus in his heart or his wife in his room.

It seemed all my life I had worked and strived, but at the age of 35 I still could not see the light at the end of the tunnel. Is this the way life is meant to be? Is life supposed to be nothing but hanging on to hopes that other men have? Is this what it's all about? A number of times I thought if this is what it's going to be like until the day I die, I would be better off dead. I also began to understand how a man could one day just disappear and leave his family and his business life. Just drop out of society. I thought I could understand the feelings of a person doing such a thing, but I knew in my own heart that I could never do it myself. You see, while I treasured our friends and family, my wife and children, I also treasured our home and our automobiles. I liked having things and wanted more—a nicer home, maybe someday even a vacation home on the ocean.

Religion was very important to me and my family. We attended church every Sunday and felt better after our attendance, but getting ourselves to church on time Sunday mornings always seemed to be somewhat stressful. I believe the devil didn't want us to go to church. We said our prayers before meals and prayed together as a family before going to bed. Cheryl, my precious wife, put together the following prayers for us to pray each night as a family, and some of our children still pray them with their families.

> Father, Son, and Holy Spirit, speak to us and let us hear it. Open our eyes, our ears, and our hearts; give us the

> chance to give you our part of love and trust and praise. Amen.
>
> God bless Mommy and Daddy; all of us children; both mamas and papas; all our aunts, uncles, cousins, and friends; and everybody in the whole world. (After this prayer we would say the Lord's Prayer.)

God was up there, I sort of believed, but you couldn't prove it by me. At the age of 35 I'd never read the Bible all the way through. Even though I had been Catholic up to that time, I don't remember ever being told to read the Bible. It was more like "Don't read the Bible; just follow the rules of the church, and that will get you to heaven." (The Catholic Church now teaches parishioners to read the Bible and promotes Bible study.) Perhaps I

> *Perhaps I was never instructed to read the Bible, even though I attended Catholic schools growing up—or maybe I was one who listened but did not hear.*

was never instructed to read the Bible, even though I attended Catholic schools growing up—or maybe I was one who listened but did not hear.

God was not real to me. I could only imagine what God might be like. God never spoke to me, no matter how much I prayed. Actually, I had never had any real personal experiences with God. I only believed because I was told to believe all my life. I had nothing personal to base my faith on, only what others had told me. So at this point in my life, with everything else in my personal life making me angry, here I was losing my faith in God. I was starting to believe that Jesus was just a good Jewish man, a prophet, as some believe.

Many who are not believers in Jesus as the Son of God and the Savior of the world say they believe that Jesus was a good man, a true prophet, but not the Son of God. What a contradiction! How can a thinking person say Jesus was just a good man and a prophet of God when He is quoted as saying, *"You are right in saying I am (the Son of God)"* in Luke 22:70–71 and *"I go to my Father"*? He says, in effect, in Matthew 7:13–14, *"I am the gate,"* and, in John 14:6 Jesus is clear: *"I am the way.*" There are thousands of words spoken by Jesus in the Bible, and He doesn't mince words. As noted, Jesus says clearly that He is the Son of God. He cannot have said what He said and just be a good man and a prophet of God. Either Jesus is who He said He is or He is a liar, a lunatic, the ultimate con man, and a hypocrite. In *Mere Christianity,* C. S. Lewis puts it this way: "Either this man was, and is, the Son of God: or else a madman or something worse."

So, as you can see, I was losing my interests, my spiritual beliefs, and I was questioning day-in, day-out striving to earn more to buy more useless material.

– 3 –

The Devil Wanted Me—and Had Me for a While

There have been many times in my life, especially when I felt I was in danger, that God came to mind. I am sure that everyone, when they know they are dying, will look to God. Yes, I think any gambler would advise you to bet on God's existence. The consequences of disbelief will last literally for eternity, as 17th-century French philosopher and mathematician Blaise Pascal stated in his famous "wager." Growing up, I believed in God in a detached sort of way. I hoped that before I died God would give me a chance to make an act of contrition for my sins. That would be my only chance at eternity with God, my only hope, because even though I tried to do no evil, I failed daily. Even now, I fail daily. I do the things I do not want to do and don't always do the things I know I should do (see Paul's words in Romans 7).

You see, I had been taught as a Catholic that there is a God who is sort of like Santa Claus. He knows everything we do, so you better watch out, you better not cry, you better not pout, and I'm telling you why: God is watching! If you do evil He will throw you into a fire for eternity, but if you confess your sins before you die, you get eternity in heaven. I learned that God was a God to fear! Fear was the major determining factor in relating to God. Fear of God is the beginning of wisdom, I was taught. (What I didn't realize at the time was that the truest definition of the Biblical word "fear"—for example, as it's used in Job 28:28—is "reverential awe, especially toward God," as the dictionary says, not fear in the sense of cowering in terror.) I began to question this kind of God in my mind, not to anyone else and not even consciously, but the devil had me doubting. The lying, cheating, pride-filled devil had a hold on me.

For a year before I gave my life to Jesus Christ, I started thinking Jesus was probably just a good Jew. Why? I didn't know Him. He never talked to me. He never impressed me with any special knowledge. To me Jesus was no more than an image that we were supposed to pray to, almost like a statue. I felt I received nothing in return. I supposed that the Christian religion was all faith and no experience. Certainly it was the best gamble, as Pascal said in his wager—much better to gamble on eternity with God than eternity in hell. Praise God, I know that was one reason I held on to my religion. That and the benefits I somehow sensed that faith would bring to my family were the only reasons. *Jesus, I thank you now.* I feel the Spirit of God in this writing. I have asked God to lead me in this, and I know He is doing just that.

During that year I seemed to have no real control over my temptations. In my sales position I traveled over many miles in many different states. Even a sensible person may do some things away from home that he wouldn't consider doing in his own town. The deceitful devil wants to tear us down just as he did Adam and Eve. The devil takes away our self-confidence, joy, and love for others; he's a thief and a liar. So I seemed to have no control over my desires. Praise God, before things got completely out of control, God touched me and changed

I found out the truth—that there is more to life and God than just tradition and words of faith.

me, and in changing me, He took away what had become an unrelenting desire for sin. God talked to me in my spirit. He showed me that He is alive and true, and He does perform miracles in our day. I found out the truth—that there is more to life and God than just tradition and words of faith. Jesus Christ is alive, and the Bible is the Word of God. Let me explain how I came to this realization—even revelation—in my life.

Here I was at age 35, burnt out on all the traveling, the material roller coaster. I was depressed, angry at my own weaknesses, no longer interested in my daily business, and I didn't know the answer to my problem. As I sat in business meetings I was bored with all the discussion and did not want to be there. I considered going to a psychiatrist but didn't give it much thought because of pride.

One weekend in 1974, I was helping folks at an elementary school in Nashville, Tennessee, set up a stand for their annual fair. They were going to serve our company's pizza at the fair. I noticed that the person at the stand next to ours was selling used books. I was and still am an avid reader, so I looked the books over. The lady selling the used books was very nice and showed me some novels that she recommended. I explained that I would prefer nonfiction, preferably stories of people's lives. Seldom do I read novels; I prefer books concerning my profession of selling, lives of successful businesspeople, and true stories of survival. She held up a book that was in bad shape, but she said she thought I would appreciate it. She showed me where her children had used crayons—on every page—but the book was readable. It was published by the Full Gospel Business Men's Association. She also showed me a book titled *A Man Called Peter,* by Catherine Marshall. The two books were only a quarter each, but I felt that wasn't enough, so I gave her extra money for the books. As I look back, I'm sure those books were meant for me at that time in my life.

The book of true success stories, by the Full Gospel Business Men's Association, was the most incredible collection of stories of very successful men who had shared their experiences of the Holy Spirit. How, in their businesses and personal lives, God had led them in their decision making and given them answers to difficult problems. How God had opened doors and closed doors in their decision making. They gave all the credit for their successes in life to God. They stated that God was their true source in all they did. The second book, *A Man Called Peter,* is a wonderful, must-read inspirational book about Peter Marshall, a true man of God.

I gave my oldest brother Don, with whom I was in business, the book by the Full Gospel Business Men's Association. At the time I gave him this book, he had been reading a book by Merlin Carothers called *Prison to Praise.* Carothers' books are easy-to-read, Spirit-filled books that I recommend to everyone. I have given away thousands of copies of Carothers' books since 1974 because his books change lives. Our entire family came to know Jesus as personal Savior because of the book *Prison to Praise.*

A few days after I gave my brother the book, I phoned a woman on business who suddenly began to tell me all her problems—and that she was thinking of killing herself that day. After the call, I mentioned this to my brother Don, and we said a prayer for her. Don asked for her name and address because he wanted to visit with her. When he returned to the office he said they had prayed together and she surrendered all her problems to God. He said by the end of their visit she was praising God! There was something different about my brother that I didn't understand at the time.

Don is my brother and a respected businessman. He thinks outside the box; you never know what he will come up with next. He's the ultimate marketing entrepreneur. Circus magnate P. T. Barnum would have loved the way he thinks. The wholesale food company that he founded under the name Pepe's Pizza was growing and doing very well financially at this time. We had a dedicated team of people working alongside us in the company. It seemed everything Don touched turned to gold. He was named an All-American in high school football and went on to Vanderbilt on a football scholarship. He was an outstanding ball carrier who was hard to tackle. He ran his business like he played football. He wouldn't go around a problem; he went right through it. This didn't always make him friends, but it got the job done.

We were brought up to know right from wrong, but our religious background was not built on personal experience; as I said earlier, it was built on tradition and the fear of going to hell. (I must say that the Catholic Church is a blessing in so many ways. I thank God for my upbringing in Catholic schools and the Catholic Church, as it led me to a lifetime of seeking God. One of the most wonderful gifts the Catholic Church offers is its daily church service. Starting the day praising God with others is so powerful.)

> *We were brought up to know right from wrong, but our religious background was not built on personal experience ...*

The day after Don's visit with the woman who surrendered to God, he asked me to come down the hall to his office for a few minutes. When I went in that morning, he shared something with me that was to change my life. My brother told me that recently he had been so depressed as a result of people problems and business decisions, as well as personal problems, that he had been seriously thinking of taking his life. He said that after reading the book I had given to him, he was angry. This book, published by the Full Gospel Business Men's Association, contained the stories of many different men who had given their lives to God and how God had changed their lives. It also told how anyone could experience the same thing. He said he was 40 years of age, and God had never spoken to him. He said he was so angry that he had told God, "I don't love you; I don't know you; I don't even know if there is a God, but after reading this book, I am going to do what these people say to do. I want what they profess to have."

Don then told me that several days earlier he had said to God, "I *will* to believe that Jesus Christ is my personal Savior. I am sorry for every wrong I ever committed in my life, and I surrender my will to your will." He said he told God he didn't love Him, but he *willed* to love Him. He surrendered his life, desires, ambitions, family, material goods, and business—everything he had and everything he would ever have—to God. Don went on to say that he felt no emotion at that moment, but the next morning he woke up praising God and had never felt so clean and good in all his life. He said to me, "I know I am saved; I am reborn, a new person."

This was exciting! I had never heard of being saved through the Catholic Church, but I had heard of being saved elsewhere—through two brothers who owned a drive-in restaurant in Chattanooga, Tennessee (some years before I had serviced their restaurant with our pizza). Now here was my Catholic brother telling me he was saved, that he was a new person, reborn.

Don had me spellbound with his story. My life wasn't rosy, and I knew I needed something. God was answering my need. Don asked me if he could pray for me. Then he asked me to kneel down, and he put one of his hands on my head. Now, this kind of touching was a bit weird for us brothers. Nevertheless, he prayed to God and asked God to take over my life, and he asked me if I would like a closer walk with God. Then he asked me to repeat after him this simple prayer:

> I believe Jesus Christ died on the cross for my sins and is my personal Savior. I am sorry for every wrong I ever committed in my life toward God or man. I surrender my life, my desires, my family, my will, my future desires, and my material goods to you, Lord. I ask you, Jesus, to take over my life and fill me with the Holy Spirit.

With a deep sense of honesty and sincerity, I repeated all of this after Don, and I know he was led by the Holy Spirit—who gives us courage to tell others the Good News. Don clearly was filled with courage. I don't remember feelings of emotion, except that I felt a very strong love toward my brother for sharing this with me. (That love was certainly toward Don, but also toward Jesus, who glowed out from my brother.) I remember that as we got up, we hugged each other, and this may have been the first time we had ever embraced. We had hugged our sisters, our mother, and any young lady who would let us, but we brothers didn't hug each other. Because of Jesus this changed, and now we hug our other brothers and our sons.

– 4 –

Angry Until God Touched Me

I woke up the next morning a changed man. Yes, I felt and knew the change. I woke up thanking Jesus in my mind and with my lips. All my life I had prayed because I, Jim Hunt, decided to pray. Now, the Holy Spirit was praising God through me. I was the same person, yet I was changed. I was reborn. In John 3 Jesus tells Nicodemus that he must be reborn—of the Holy Spirit—to be saved.

I remembered the two brothers who operated a drive-in restaurant in Chattanooga called Pop's. Every week when I serviced them with pizza, they would try to share something from the Bible with me. They even asked me if I was saved. I had no idea what they meant. Because I had been told I was in the one and only true church, the Catholic Church, I was proud of the fact that I didn't have to go around looking for a church. In fact, I never had any desire to read the Bible because I believed that my spiritual life was being taken care of by the Catholic Church. (Readings at Catholic services are of Scripture from the Bible; daily the Bible is read at services.)

> *I told them I thanked God that I didn't have to worry about the Bible and could spend my time and energy trying to make a living. I told them I didn't talk religion or politics.*

One day these two restaurant owners were trying to show me passages in the Bible explaining why we need to be saved. I felt like I was being pressured. So, very all-knowingly, I told them I was happy being a Catholic. I told them I thanked God that I didn't have to worry about the Bible and could spend my time and energy trying to make a living. I told them I didn't talk religion or politics. (Ignorance is not bliss, I assure you. We must pray for wisdom.) After that, if I remember correctly, they left me to my ignorance. Probably they gave up on me, yet knowing they had at least planted some seeds in my heart. And I'm sure they prayed for me. I appreciate and love these two brothers. They were and are apostles for Jesus Christ.

After 35 years of life, the only men I can remember having talked to me about being reborn through faith in Jesus Christ are these two restaurant owners and my brother Don. To be perfectly fair before God and my teachers, I should note that the Bible (Isaiah 6 and Matthew 13) says some will listen but will not hear. How dense can man be? I studied for 12 years in the Catholic school system. Did I miss the Word, or did my teachers miss something?

The Living Bible, a paraphrased version of Scripture, had become available by this time, when I was developing a strong desire to read the Word of God. It's the most amazing thing: When you surrender your life to Jesus, reading the Word of God becomes very important. But while I did read the Bible, I also read every book I could get my hands on by other born-again Christians. Actually I never read the whole

Bible through. Instead of reading the Bible completely, I was reading other books about Jesus and books about the lives of Christians.

One day, Bill Davis, a brother in Christ in our company, came into my office and said he'd had a dream about me. He said he was led to conclude that I should read the Bible and quit reading so many other books. (The Spirit of God works in so many wondrous ways.) Bill's account of his dream impressed me, but not so strongly that I was going to put the book I was reading aside and go to the Bible immediately.

On the way home that night, I stopped at a grocery store. While I was waiting in line to pay, I stood behind an older man who was buying about 15 packages of candy and cookies. I sized him up as an addict who was on sweets instead of booze. His bill for all of this was about $10 (in 1974). I mentioned to him how expensive everything was, and very quickly he turned around, looked me in the eyes, and said, "You know what? The only book you can believe is the Bible." That apparent *non sequitur* was all he said to me, and he turned around, picked up his bag of goodies, and left the

> *"You know what? The only book you can believe is the Bible."*

store! He left *me* with my mouth hanging open; this was pretty unbelievable. Two different people in two days were telling me to read the Bible. As I left to get into my car, I noticed he was out in the lot going through his pockets as though he had lost something. While I was driving out of the lot, he turned around and headed back for the store. About that time it occurred to me that this man could use some money, and I suddenly realized God had worked through him to give me a message. I turned around, and as I drove back into the lot, this angel of God was walking across the lot, and we met just right. Reaching out the window with a 20-dollar bill, I said, "I would like to give you this money and thank you for giving me the message about the Bible." He said, "Thank you. I really can use the money." God used us both to meet a need. The only thing we need to do is listen and follow His leading—discern His will in every moment of our lives.

After the spiritual change in my life, I had an urgency to say the name of Jesus to everyone I met. The name Jesus is so powerful that just saying the name can change lives.

The very next morning after my encounter with the man at the grocery store, I was on my way to the office and running late, when I saw a man sitting in front of a shack-type business in a chair reading something. He had his chair tilted back against the front wall of the shack. I had seen him before and was curious as to what he was selling from that shack.

My intention after satisfying my curiosity was to somehow say the name of Jesus, if possible, to this man. I walked over to him, introduced myself, and asked what he was selling. He explained that he sold automobile tire planters. While he was showing me the tires, he asked me to help him turn one inside out. Now, I was on my way to the office and had on a suit and a white shirt and tie, but I helped him turn the tire inside out. He was able to get tires that were to be thrown away and cut them in half like a bagel, then he notched them on the edges with a knife and turned them inside out. He painted them all different colors—but mostly red, white, and blue. People bought them for their yards to encircle their flowers or bushes. After looking over the others he had for sale, we talked a bit, and I said I would stop again sometime. At one point we introduced ourselves to each other—and Mr. Newkirk asked me how old I thought he was. I had no idea but guessed he was in his 60s. He smiled and said he was 90 years old. He was truly a healthy, handsome man with bright eyes and a young face. Then he said, "Let me give you something." He went into the shack and brought out a leaflet and handed it to me. I looked at the outside and put it in my pocket; nothing on the outside told me much.

I left Mr. Newkirk and got into my car. He then came around my car and stuck his hand in the window. I assumed he wanted to shake my hand, so I took his. He said, "Could we say a prayer together?" I couldn't begin to tell you my feelings. His prayer was beautiful. He thanked God that He had sent me to be his prayer partner. He ended his prayer saying, "In the name of Jesus Christ"—exactly what I had intended to say to him. God let him show me how simple it was to pray with someone and say the name above all names, Jesus.

> *God is so good to His children.*

God is so good to His children. After I left Mr. Newkirk, I looked at the leaflet and discovered it had a postcard attached that I could fill out to receive free Bible lessons. Wow! You'd better believe I started reading more of the Bible and less of the other books. I signed up for those free Bible lessons also. Jesus is alive, and the Bible is the Word of God. The Spirit of God is available to each of us, but it's up to us to turn our will over to Jesus. No one can do it for us. We have a free will. It's our choice.

Many wonderful things have happened in the time since I surrendered my life to the Lord. Many wonderful miracles can happen daily if we trust His will and follow His Word. You see, Jesus will speak to us if we listen. (Had anyone told me this a few years ago, I would have classified that person as a nut.) Jesus is the same yesterday, today, and forever. Take a minute and think about what that means: The power, wisdom, and love that Jesus brought to the world have never changed. The things

Jesus does today are the same as those He did when He was on this earth—but now they're through you and me, through people who follow His will. We all can have His power if we surrender to His will.

– 5 –

A Road Trip to Gatlinburg

One morning shortly after I had given my life to Jesus, my brother Don came to my office and told me that he believed the Holy Spirit had told him to go to Gatlinburg, Tennessee, with Bill Davis and me. Bill had recently come to the Lord as well. We three went home, packed up, and left for Gatlinburg. On the trip we went out of our way and stopped at a church off the highway and picked up three songbooks. (Yes, we permanently "borrowed" them because I guess we thought it was for a good cause!) So here we were, three guys driving down the highway singing praises to God. We had never sung together before, and not one of us could carry a tune. It was pretty hilarious, but it was meaningful to us (and, I hope, to the Lord!). Normally we would be talking about our business, but not on this journey.

We arrived in Gatlinburg around 8 p.m.; since it was winter, it was dark. We had not made hotel reservations and had nothing in mind except that we wanted a fireplace in our room. We wanted to stay where Jesus wanted us to stay, so we pulled over to the side of the road and said a prayer asking God to lead us where He wanted us to stay. There were hundreds of motels, chalets, and condominiums in the Gatlinburg area, but as I said, we wanted to be where God wanted us to be.

We drove on farther to the end of Gatlinburg's main street and saw a chalet rental office on our left. We drove over and saw a "Closed" sign on the door, but we noticed there was a light on in the back area of the building, and there was a man at a desk. We knocked on the door and asked him if he could rent a chalet to us. He explained that he was a surveyor and just shared the office with the rental staff but said he would phone Mack Reed, who owned the rental business, and see if a chalet might be available. He was able to get Mr. Reed on the phone, so we shared with him how we came to be in Gatlinburg and that we had prayed for a place to stay. We told him we felt that God had led us to his office. He appreciated what we said, told us he would get our information the next day, and instructed the surveyor to give us the key to a chalet. The one we were to stay in for two nights was already rented to others the third night, but Mr. Reed, a man we had never met, invited us to stay at his home if we decided to stay longer than two nights. This was certainly not the normal thing a property owner would say to strangers. God is so good to His children. We stopped and bought some cheddar cheese and other things, then headed up to the chalet.

We started a fire in the fireplace and sat around it singing Christian songs. The next morning we woke up early and ate a little something. We sat out on the balcony enjoying the beautiful Smoky Mountains and talking about Jesus and our new outlook on life. We discussed our business, and the day went by quickly. Around 5 p.m. we started talking about getting some dinner. Restaurants are everywhere in Gatlinburg, so we drove down into town to find a place to eat. As we drove through town we passed at least 30 restaurants, but no one recommended eating at any of them. One of us suggested we say a prayer and ask where God wanted us to eat. His way is

> *There is wisdom in asking the Lord for direction before making decisions.*

always the best way. There is wisdom in asking the Lord for direction before making decisions.

We drove straight through town and came out the other end in Pigeon Forge. All of a sudden my brother made an abrupt right turn and then almost immediately turned left into a church parking lot. He said he didn't know what happened; he just felt led to turn and didn't feel he had a choice. There was a man sitting in a car in front of the church. Don got out of our car, walked over to the man, and asked him if there was a service that evening. The man said there wasn't any service scheduled for that night. My brother then asked him why he was sitting in the parking lot. The man said he was the pastor of the church and had called a meeting with the elders to discuss something that was personally very important to him. The meeting was scheduled for an hour earlier, but no one had showed up. He said he had just been sitting there waiting and praying for the last hour. We asked if we could go inside the church and pray with him. He said he would appreciate our prayers, so all four of us went into the church.

He told us that the elders of the church weren't happy with his conduct as pastor. He wanted to preach on the sidewalks of Gatlinburg and have healing services. He wanted to be led in his ministry by the Holy Spirit. The elders had let him know that they were not in agreement with this type of ministry. He wanted to meet with them that evening to discuss these matters in order to be able to decide if he should leave his position as pastor of the church.

We four knelt at the communion rail and prayed together that God would give him the wisdom and courage to do what God wanted him to do. As we stood up, the man thanked us for following the prompting of the Spirit by approaching him in the parking lot. We then asked him where he would suggest we have our dinner, and immediately he gave us the name of a restaurant that had home-cooked meals right there in Pigeon Forge.

We walked into the restaurant and sat down and studied the menu. We had only had some cheddar cheese that morning and hadn't eaten the night before, so we were hungry. The waitress took Bill's order and mine, but when it came time for Don to order, he said he didn't feel like eating. Then he got up and walked around the room. He started talking to people at a table on the other side of the room, then went over and looked at some cards on a rack. He came back with one of the cards and gave it to me, saying this must be for me. Don said he then was hungry and ordered his meal. He told us that when he walked into the restaurant he felt there was something important he was supposed to do. He believed that the message on the card he had found was meant for me.

2011

I am writing this in 2011. I was given the card in 1974, and it is still on my bathroom mirror in my office. This is how the card reads:

> ***A Prayer for Today***
> *by Richard M. "Pek" Gunn, Poet Laureate of Tennessee*
>
> "Blessed Are the Pure in Heart, for They Shall See God"

Give me a heart so pure that I
Will see my God in everything.
Not only in the prosperous days,
But in reverses life may bring.
A heart submissive to his will
When sunny days give way to rain;
Such blessings count of equal worth
As those based on material gain.
A heart that clings, though paths are dim,
And cherished hopes have turned to dust,
A heart so fixed, though slain by him,
Will still give praise and dare to trust.

1975

For some unknown reason while we were eating I kept saying, “When I get back to the chalet, I am going to get under the bed.” It made no sense, but we laughed about it because I said it so much. The food and the service were excellent. God had answered our prayer asking for a place to enjoy delicious, down-home country fixin’s.

We left the restaurant around 9 p.m. and headed back through Gatlinburg toward our chalet. I was still saying I was going to get under the bed when I got to the chalet. As we passed Mr. Reed's chalet rental office, which was on the way to our chalet, we saw the young man, the surveyor, working in his office at this late hour. We pulled over to turn around, but first we stopped and said a prayer to ask God whether we should go over and talk to him. We were questioning why he was in his office so late again.

We went to the door; he saw us and let us in. We told him we were surprised to see him again working so late and asked if there was something we could pray about with him. He took a deep breath, then told us he had just that evening received divorce papers from his wife—as he held up the papers. He said with sincerity that he didn't even know there was a problem. We asked him if we could pray with him, and he said he would really appreciate our prayers. All of us held hands and prayed that the young man and his wife could work this out and not divorce. We asked him if he would like to surrender his life to Jesus. He surrendered his life to Jesus that night and made Jesus Lord of his life.

We left his office and drove up toward the chalet. As we approached the chalet, I saw a man standing at the door of the lower level with his hand on the doorknob. He was wearing black pants and a white dress shirt. I told Bill and Don what I saw, but they didn't see him. We hadn't met Mack Reed, the owner of the chalet rental company, so I thought it might be Mack.

We parked the car and looked around but saw no one. We entered the chalet, and Bill and Don were concerned that the person I saw could have been an intruder, so we looked under all the beds and in all the rooms and closets. We checked the doors, and all were locked. There didn't seem to be any disturbance. The unusual part of this was that I had no fear about the person I had seen at the lower-level door. I was at peace with the situation. Later that evening, as I thought about it more, I believed the man was an angel, but both Bill and Don were uneasy about the stranger's apparent presence so close to us.

We made a fire in the fireplace, and Bill suggested we kneel down and say a prayer. We knelt and asked God to protect us. Suddenly we heard a noise, a banging noise, coming from the fireplace. The noise sounded like someone hitting metal with a hammer. It stopped and then started again. This time it was coming from a plastic basket next to the fireplace that held kindling wood. The noise stopped for a couple of minutes and started again but came from the bathroom. We said a prayer asking God what this meant. Suddenly it was even louder, coming from the fireplace again, like someone banging metal with a sledgehammer. One of us said, "Father, what does this mean?" and Bill said very solemnly, "Go home!" We quickly stood, and all agreed that we should go home immediately.

We put the money we owed the rental company on the counter and left Mack Reed a note explaining why we had to leave. We left the place and headed home around 10 p.m. We were in such a hurry that we left a nice block of aged sharp cheddar cheese in the refrigerator.

While driving back to Nashville that evening, we discussed what had happened over that day and a half. We agreed that God had worked through us and that the ones we prayed for may have thought we were angels. We believed that God had sent us to the pastor, the surveyor, and Mack Reed. That is how much God loves His children. God is so good to His children.

I arrived home about 2 a.m. and my sweet Cheryl was so happy to see me that I knew we had done the right thing coming home. Cheryl was and is my gift from God. There is nothing as wonderful as a woman who loves you regardless of your faults and is invariably loving and supportive of you.

– 6 –

STP

ABOUT A YEAR LATER, WHEN I resigned from Pepe's Pizza and moved to Gatlinburg, I again met the pastor; he also had resigned and was now the pastor of another church, doing what the Holy Spirit led him to do. While I lived in Gatlinburg, five of us men met weekly for Bible study and prayer, including this pastor. I ended up renting a chalet for a year from Mack Reed and took part in many conversations and prayers with him and his family. I even helped him and his men cut firewood to supply his rental chalets.

My reason for sharing my inner thoughts, my soul, with you is that you may see a life before it was touched by the living God. My hope is that no one should have to wait until the age of 35 before knowing this inner peace that is available by surrendering, trusting, and praising God daily.

Surrender, trust, and *praise* have become an important part of my everyday life. I remember when my brother Don one day told me the Holy Spirit had given him this gift to share with others. It is a life-changer and, by thinking STP, it is simple to remember. My reason for writing this is that your children may be raised to know the Good News: Because Jesus died on the cross, we can have eternal life, Jesus is alive today, and the Bible is the Word of God.

> Surrender, trust, *and* praise *have become an important part of my everyday life. ... This gift to share with others ... is a life-changer and, by thinking STP, it is simple to remember.*

The denomination of the church you choose to attend makes little difference, so long as you are being fed from the Bible and Jesus is Lord. If you have not surrendered your life to Jesus and will to do so now, just pray the prayer below, telling God you *will* to believe this on faith and you want this peace in your life.

> Jesus, I believe you died for my sins—past, present, and future—and, because you died, I will know life for eternity.
>
> I am sorry for all my sins and for any wrong or wrongs I have ever done against anyone. If possible I will make right whatever I have done to hurt anyone. I forgive everyone who has ever done anything negative to me.
>
> I surrender everything I have to you—my family, my business, my desires, my hopes and dreams, my home, and all my material things.
>
> I ask that you take over my life and make me one with you. Thank you, Jesus.

After sincerely praying the above words you may or may not have feelings of emotion. Feelings are not necessary with God. If your prayer was genuine and came from the heart, you are now a follower of Jesus Christ. You are a new person, and Jesus is Lord of your life. Start reading the Bible daily, beginning with the books of John and Acts. You will be blessed as you read and come to know the peace of God through His Word.

A few years ago I borrowed a book from Bill Schindler, my stepfather, who married my mother 20 years after my father died. In the book was a poem from a newspaper he had saved.

The Calf Path
by Sam Walter Foss, 1985

One day thru the primeval wood
A calf walked home, as good calves should;
But made a trail, as all calves do.
Since then 300 years have fled,
And I infer the calf is dead.
But still, he left behind his trail
And thereby hangs my mortal tale.

The trail was taken up next day
By a lone dog that passed that way.
And then, a wise bellwether sheep
Pursued the trail, o'er vale and steep.
And drew the flocks behind him too
As good bellwethers always do.
And from that day, o'er hill and glade,
Thru those old woods, a path was made.

And many men wound in and out
And dodged, and turned, and bent about
And uttered words of righteous wrath
Because 'twas such a crooked path,
But still they followed, do not laugh,
The first migrations of that calf.

And thru the winding woods they stalked
Because he wobbled when he walked.
This forest path became a lane

That bent, and turned, and turned again.
This crooked lane became a road
Where many a poor horse with his load
Toiled on beneath the burning sun
And traveled some three miles in one.
And thus a century and a half
They trod the footsteps of that calf.

The years passed on in swiftness fleet,
The road became a village street.
And this, before men were aware,
A city's crowded thoroughfare.
And soon the central street was this
Of a renowned metropolis,
Trod in the footsteps of that calf.

Each day a hundred thousand rout
Followed the zigzag calf about,
And o'er his crooked journey went
The traffic of a continent.

A hundred thousand men were led
By one calf, near three centuries dead.
They followed still his crooked way
And lost a hundred years per day.
For thus such reverence is lent
To well-established precedent.

A moral lesson this might teach
Were I ordained, and called to preach.
For men are prone to go it blind
Along the calf paths of the mind,
And some work away from sun to sun
To do what other men have done.
They follow in the beaten track
And out and in, and forth and back.
And still their devious course pursue
To keep the paths that others do.

They keep the paths a sacred groove
Along which all their lives they move.
But how the wise old wood gods laugh
Who saw that first primeval calf.
Ah, many things this tale might teach,
But I am not ordained to preach.

This is the way I was, just being led down the path by those before me. This is the way many of us are. We follow the beliefs of our parents or our church, or we go into the professions of our parents, just because those are the easiest paths to follow. We don't take the time to pray and decide what we really believe, what God wants us to do with our lives.

The following erupted out of me one day when I was thinking about how empty life was before God touched me.

1974

Who knows the loneliness of my heart, the emptiness of my life? The burning, churning emptiness of a man who knows not God? A lonely man has yet to see his worth in life as it can be; a man who knows not God is not a whole man.

For a man who knows not God, there seems no plan. God alone will guide your life exactly as it should be. God the Father gave us His Son, who died and gave us everlasting life, but you must believe to receive this free gift.

Believing to receive is so easy; why do so many choose not to believe?

When your time comes, and you are lying there dying, then I suspect you will want to believe.

Don't wait until your dying moment to receive the love of our Lord. Your life on earth has so much in store if you will only surrender right where you are.

You see, Jesus Christ did die for our sins and gave us everlasting life.

The Good News is that it is free.

When we surrender our lives and our wills, the resulting inner peace surpasses that of anything else on this earth.

– 7 –

Surrender

WHAT NOW FOLLOWS WAS WRITTEN in 1974 shortly after I gave my life to the Lord. I was bubbling over with His love. There is nothing like it in the whole world. There is an inner strength and inner peace, a knowing that you are going to be with God for eternity. It's like a heavy weight has been taken off your shoulders, and it frees you from always having to prove yourself to yourself and to others. Your life is new, with a newness that is glorious. Let me share this with you. You will see how I surrendered my life completely to God's will.

1974

Jesus Christ, thank you.
Praise and thanks to my God.

Comforter of all, I adore you.
Christ in me is my all.

Your endless wish is my command;
My time on earth is in your hands.
Christ, my king, rule my life
To show me love as love should be.

For time is naught, time is free,
When man is filled with love from thee.
Teach me your love, my Lord,
To share with others for eternity.

Only you, Lord, know my soul;
Only you, Lord, know my will.
Life has meaning only, Lord,
When you have my will.

Take my will, take my life,
All my possessions, all my rights.
To you, Lord, I surrender my all,
And I sit at your feet in awe.

Make me pauper, make me king;
Not my will, but your will be done.
Use my body, use my mind;
Let this unworthy servant be your vine.

God is good to us. He has so many wonders for us to enjoy. Do we take the time to thank Him for all the wonders around us? In 1975 I wrote what appears below, through the

Holy Spirit, I am sure. Through the years I have come to the conclusion that these words were given *to* me and were meant *for* me. This message has taught me to be thankful; I have developed the habit of thanking Jesus for another day, for my wife and children, for a way to care for my family financially, and for each of the wonderful people who operate our business. I thank Jesus for my parents, my brothers and sisters, and all the family members of my precious Cheryl. I thank Jesus for my health; for being able to walk; for sight, hearing, taste, and touch; and for being able to love others. I thank Jesus for my praying aunts and uncles. I thank Jesus for all my nephews and nieces, who are such a blessing in our lives. There is no end to the things we can thank Jesus for, and I especially thank Jesus for dying on the cross and giving us eternal life.

1975

> ***Jesus Christ Loves You and Will Never Give Up on You!***
>
> No matter what you do to yourself, to your loved ones, to your enemies, Jesus Christ loves you and will never give up on you. His love is always reaching out to you.

All you must do to receive this love is accept His love. Say this now, say it out loud if possible: "Thank you, Jesus. I accept your love. I accept your will for my life."

Jesus Christ died for your sins and thereby gave you eternal life. Now tell our Lord you accept His free gift of eternal life, and surrender your will to His will.

All through the day repeat over and over, "Thank you, Jesus," and Jesus will give you inner peace, which will surpass your most cherished earthly dreams.

Jesus Christ is alive today, and the Bible is the Word of God. Acknowledge your need, accept Him into your life, and change your world. Read the Word of God daily, and learn the truth.

2011

About a year after I surrendered my life to the Lord, through circumstances out of the ordinary that had to be motivated by God, I resigned from the company I had worked with for nine years: my brother's company. The pressure I was experiencing and being burnt out on all the meetings and travel must have contributed to the decision. I gave 30 days' notice and planned to move my family to Gatlinburg, Tennessee, and write for a living. I believed the Holy Spirit was leading me to write in such a way that people who normally would not read spiritual material would pick up my books, see the power of their Savior while reading them, and give their wills (their very lives) to His charge.

My precious wife, Cheryl, was with me 100%. She never doubted this was the right move. We had three children, we had a mortgage and automobile debt, and even though she knew we would have no income, she was with me completely! We wrote Mack Reed's rental chalet company in Gatlinburg, asking for help finding a place to live there. Mack bought and sold properties. One year earlier he had rented Bill, Don, and me a chalet in Gatlinburg by phone only on our word. At the time of our move, I still had not met Mack, but I knew him as a friend because of the way he treated us the year before. We hired a Christian Realtor to help us sell our home in Nashville. We prayed together each time we met. In just six days our home sold for exactly the price we had listed it for.

That year, in 1975, Mack and Betty Reed became our very good friends. They offered us a chalet that we could rent, which was a better arrangement for us than buying a home. When

Cheryl and I saw the chalet, we thought it was beautiful, and it was especially wonderful considering that we had prepared ourselves for whatever minimal accommodations God had for us. There was a lovely stone fireplace, much nicer than the one we left in Nashville. A balcony wrapped around the entire chalet. It had four bedrooms; one, which had a terrific view, could be used for me to write. The chalet had an upstairs master bedroom with its own outside balcony and an inside balcony looking down on the living room. Off our balcony were a waterfall and creek that splashed and gurgled—and were music to our ears. The evergreens and other trees were so tall that they reached above the balconies. This place had seven sets of sliding doors. We were happy and thanked God for this home. Mack and Betty offered us an exceptionally low rent for the year, and 75% of the year's rent could be applied to the purchase price if we decided to buy later. The most important thing for me was that Cheryl was happy with our new home.

For three months Cheryl, the children, and I just enjoyed each other and nature. I believed that when it was time to write, God would give me the words. We knew we were in God's will, and we read God's Word daily. We knew that anything that happened was part of His will, and only good could come from His will. Shortly after we arrived in Gatlinburg we discovered Cheryl was pregnant with our fourth child. Our son Todd Austin was born that year, and even though finances were low, it was a life-changing year.

One day I was in the woods cutting a dead pine tree for firewood. At that time in my life I had no experience with a chainsaw. I wasn't raised in the city or in the country; I was raised somewhere in between. We just didn't have any need for a chainsaw where I grew up. So that entire year I cut our firewood with an axe. I cut only dead trees that were down. It was healthy exercise.

That day the thought came to me that unless I swung that axe and cut that wood and carried it home, I wouldn't have any firewood. Unless I went out to get firewood, I wouldn't have any to burn. I had to *find, cut,* and *pick up* the firewood. I immediately thanked God out loud. God had shown me that just as I had to pick up the axe and start to cut, I had to pick up my pen and start to write.

It is true that we are to pray and ask God to lead us and help us in our decision making, but *we* must take the next step toward our purpose. The *action* of taking that step forward is most important. There have been times when I needed to make a major decision. Each time, I have asked God to help me make the decision that would be right for all involved. It has amazed me how God cares about our human needs. Many times after praying about a decision, the right way to proceed has become very clear. Sometimes opportunities or plans I've thought were so good have just become unavailable, as though a door were closing. Other times doors have opened in such a way that I've known God was showing me the right way. It was and is a miracle how God does answer when we ask.

Now I know you would like to hear that I succeeded in my writing, but the truth is that this is 2011, and much of what you are reading I wrote in Gatlinburg in 1975. I believe God wanted me to write *It's Time to Change Your Values,* but I never did write that book. I did write some things that year and sent them off to magazines and publishers, but I never sold one. Now in 2011 I am writing *From Dawn to Dusk,* which has

There is no free lunch in life, but effort brings rewards.

come about because I've learned another lesson about writing. A person who wants to write must set aside so many hours a day for writing and adhere to that schedule. A person who wants to be an outstanding salesman must put in the time to develop his talents. You want to be an outstanding athlete? You must put in the necessary time daily to train. There is no free lunch in life, but effort brings rewards. I may have understood the first lesson of *finding, cutting,* and *picking up,* but it took me some time before I understood this second lesson of *adherence.*

The year we lived in Gatlinburg was a wonderful, transformative year. We especially cherish our relationship with my cousin Otto Preske and his wife, JoAnne. Otto and JoAnne moved to Gatlinburg during the year we were there and developed a very successful business. He is known in Gatlinburg as the "Artist in Wood." His woodwork is all over the world. In addition to deepening our relationship with Otto and JoAnne, Cheryl and I had the opportunity to make many new friends with people who came to Gatlinburg, as we did, in order to draw closer to God. It seems the mountains draw people for that purpose. We enjoyed good, simple food like homemade biscuits, sausage and gravy, delicious fresh-dough pizza, homemade cinnamon rolls, and loaves of sourdough bread. We hiked all over the Smoky Mountains. I know our stay added years to my life and was a highlight of our marriage.

After the year in Gatlinburg my other two brothers, Lonnie (older) and Charlie (younger), invited me to start my own wholesale pizza business within their business area in north-central Kentucky (Louisville area). They were willing to share their area with me. After studying the area, I believed they were being too generous and truly didn't need another brother competitor. All three of my brothers have been my closest friends through the years. All three of them have been my mentors and are truly a blessing to me. In 1976, after visiting Lonnie and Charlie, I started a business in Paris, Kentucky, just northeast of Lexington in the eastern part of the state. I had no money. My sister Mary mailed me $700, which allowed me to move our things to Paris. Mary later told me the $700 was all she had in savings, but God told her to send it. I borrowed $6,000 from the bank I had dealt with in Nashville to buy a van and pay our first month's rent of $300. I believe God led my family into its own wholesale pizza business based in Paris. Over the years, from 1976 to the present, we have grown into 28 states, and more than 6,500 partners now sell Hunt Brothers Pizza. We have been blessed to have some of the most self-motivated and enthusiastic people you'll ever meet involved in our business. We give God all the glory and share what is His already with those in need.

We have grown into 28 states, and more than 6,500 partners now sell Hunt Brothers Pizza.

In 1990 we four brothers—Don, Lonnie, Jim, and Charlie—came together and formed what is now known as Hunt Brothers Pizza. We agreed that we would grow our business using principles given to us in the Word of God. These Biblical principles are taught in our company training schools and continually ingrained in our people through the "Culture" division of Hunt Brothers Pizza led by my daughter Erin Ferguson.

OUR GUIDING PRINCIPLES

Place God first in all we do,
Be a blessing to people,
Trust God to meet our needs,
Strive for excellence.

– 8 –

As the Twig Is Bent, So Grows the Tree: My Early Years in Work and Business

Becoming a successful businessman, by the grace of God, was a long and arduous journey. Yet I had countless early experiences, even as a child, that pointed me in the direction of a business career. But in those early years, of course, I had no idea that God—and my brothers—eventually would be my partners.

I was born August 5, 1939, in Evansville, Indiana. During the time before I was 9 years old my father, who owned and operated a very successful restaurant on Highway 41, would at different times bring home a sack full of pennies and ask me to put them into penny sleeves. Invariably he would leave some nickels, dimes, and sometimes a quarter in the bag. He

> *He said if you find anything other than pennies, they are yours. So I learned at an early age about* incentive *in relation to money.*

said if you find anything other than pennies, they are yours. So I learned at an early age about *incentive* in relation to money.

When I was 7 or 8 years old the streets of Evansville would often flood when it rained so my brothers and I would push the cars that got stuck out of the water; the drivers would give us some change.

Around age 9 I began cutting my neighbors' grass with a push mower and trimming their sidewalks. When it snowed in the winter, I shoveled snow for some cash.

Also when I was 9 my father let me work at his restaurant (Austin's) in the summertime. My first job was defrosting chest freezers and cleaning the outside of the freezers. I remember the first one he gave me to do. I told him I was finished and asked what else I could do. Dad inspected my work and said, "Son, give it another shot, then call me when it's clean." I learned from my father that he meant for me to do it right the first time. I graduated from just cleaning and defrosting freezers to sweeping floors and cleaning the storage room to peeling potatoes (lots of potatoes!) and cutting them up for fries.

Around 10 years of age I moved to washing dishes. By this time I was working eight hours a day in the summer. The dishes just kept coming, along with lots of pots and pans.

As I recall, around age 11 I was trained by my two older brothers to work the fountain. As a fountain boy at Austin's you were *the man*. I whipped up every kind of sundae, milk shakes and malts, dipped ice cream, fountain drinks, and lemonade and tea. The whole place would have fallen apart without a good fountain boy. We wore the hat that was famous for fountain boys in the 1950s.

One day my father asked (told!) me to go wait on a middle-aged man. I had been in my own little world working the fountain and didn't really face customers. I was shaking in my boots, but I still waited on the man and took the food to him.

After he had eaten, Dad told me to go back over and ask him if he might like a piece of apple, cherry, or pecan pie. The man ordered apple pie. Dad then told me to go back and ask him whether he would like some cheese on the pie—or whether he wanted the pie warmed up with a dip of ice cream on it. The customer wanted it warmed up and, yes, he wanted it *à la mode,* which meant with ice cream on top. Wow! From that moment on I became a believer in asking either/or questions instead of yes/no questions, and it led me into sales the rest of my life.

I grew up Roman Catholic and in the eighth grade, with the encouragement of a wonderful Benedictine nun, I believed I wanted to become a priest, so I left home and started attending St. Meinrad Seminary about 50 miles east of Evansville. I was home in the summer and, while home, I usually worked at the restaurant. One summer I worked for H. A. Woods Company. This was a drug store chain that my father had worked for during the Great Depression. My father managed the fountains for all of H. A. Woods' stores. Dad told me to tell H. A. Woods who I was, and this would help me to get the fountain job. Dad was right; it didn't hurt that I was James Austin Hunt's son. Sometimes, as the saying goes, it's not just *what* you know, it's *who* you know. Working for H. A. Woods was an enjoyable experience.

While attending the seminary in my junior year at the age of 16, my father, who was just 46, died from heart failure. Dad left a $10,000 life insurance policy that covered the new dining room he had recently installed at the restaurant. He left a home paid for and no other debt. He also left seven children—the oldest 21 and the youngest a year old.

The most valuable gift our father left us was the love he had showed us, the importance of integrity, the importance of God in our lives, and how to work. Dad did not leave us millions of dollars, but he taught us how to provide for ourselves. After grieving his unexpected and untimely death, the family pulled together and took on the responsibility of running the restaurant as our main source of income.

So at age 16—in the middle of my junior year—I left St. Meinrad and began attending Memorial Catholic High School in Evansville. I would work at the restaurant from 4 or 5 in

Many a night we would sit at the counter, and Don would teach me how to figure the costs and gross profits of our products and the financials of the company.

the afternoon until 11 p.m. Monday through Friday—and then on the weekends eight hours each day. So in addition to being a high school student, I also averaged more than 45 hours a week at the restaurant. My brother Don would relieve me at 11 most weekday evenings (the restaurant closed at 2 a.m.), and many a night we would sit at the counter, and Don would teach me how to figure the costs and gross profits of our products and the financials of the company. During this time I made strawberry glaze, homemade chili, breaded onion rings, breaded tenderloins, biscuits, sausage and gravy, and much more.

Lonnie, Don, and I managed the restaurant together during my last 1½ years of high school. Lonnie is a true business thinker. He is more like our father than any of us. In the last year of Dad's life he depended on Lonnie to run the business since Don was finishing up his senior year at Vanderbilt University and Dad's health was starting to fail. As a senior in high school, Lonnie was running a business, playing football, and managing more than 40 employees who were mostly older than he. I learned much from this brother during those years—and I still do.

After high school I attended college in Tampa, Florida, for two years. While in college I worked the "graveyard shift" in the American Canning Factory from 10 at night to 6 in the morning. I also worked for a dairy company moving products to the front in grocery stores. I even worked for the Joseph Schlitz company for 10 days as a tour guide for its new brewery in Tampa. One summer I stayed in Tampa, where I worked as a lifeguard, instead of going home to Evansville.

During this time (late 1950s) my two older brothers built a new Austin's restaurant in Nashville, Tennessee. They were working on another restaurant in Evansville to lease and change over to a second Austin's. At 19 I managed the second

Austin's in Evansville for a year when we decided the lease was just too much. We were working for the lessor at the rate we paid. I then worked with Lonnie at the original Austin's "Drive Up" Restaurant until I received my draft notice in 1961. I was 21 when I received it and chose the Marine Corps instead of the Army. At that time I was overweight and figured the Marines would get me in shape. They did. By the end of boot camp I had dropped 30 pounds and was in great shape.

While in the Marine Corps for four years and three months, I worked many different jobs (see bottom of next page). The Vietnam War was dramatically escalating near the time I was scheduled to get out of the Marines, so they extended my hitch three more months, but I never saw combat.

My first year in the Marines I was in California, Okinawa, Japan, China, Taiwan, Hawaii, and the Philippines. I was enlisted, and my job was in the infantry. I was a "grunt," and they also called us Marines "jarheads." Eventually, I was promoted to squad leader. Toward the end of the first year I was assigned to S-4, which is Logistics. S-4 is responsible for all supplies to the troops, which included helicopters, trucks, weapons and ammunition, all clothing, helmets and gear, food to the field, and loading the ships. On returning to California, I stayed in S-4 for a year and then moved to Motor Transport. I drove jeeps for the officers, then moved into the administrative office of Motor Transport. Within that year I became the Motor Transport Chief with the responsibility for the maintenance of all the jeeps, trucks, and trailers of the battalion. (Naturally the mechanics did the mechanical work.)

The commanding officer of Motor Transport became a good friend, and he helped me get into Special Services, the department of the military where the athletic teams operate, along with the Marine Corps Band and the lifeguards. My first position in Special Services was teaching Marines to swim and how to jump off the side of a ship if it ever became necessary. Imagine jumping off the side of a cruise ship; the aircraft carriers and destroyers are just as high. After this I was able to get transferred to a lifeguard position on the officers' beach in Oceanside, California.

During my time in the Marines I also worked at a Shakey's Pizza Parlor, a men's clothing store, a taco chain, and a restaurant like Waffle House. In addition, I did some sales for Success Motivation Institute out of Waco, Texas. Finally, I took flying lessons and earned my pilot's license.

After being honorably discharged from the Marines in early 1966, I stayed in California for three months doing sales work for Success Motivation Institute, strictly on commission. But I was having a hard time making enough presentations to support myself, plus I was homesick for my family. So in April of '66 I drove from Oceanside, California, to Nashville, Tennessee, and began working with Don, Lonnie, and Charlie in the Wholesale Pizza Company. While I was in the Marines my brothers had leased out the original Austin's and were no longer in the restaurant business. They were in the wholesale pizza business and wanted me to join them. At the time they were doing around $3,000 worth of business a week.

From 1966 to 1975 I helped develop the Wholesale Pizza Company, which became Pepe's Pizza Company. By 1975 Pepe's was in 20 states. My responsibilities during those years were sales, troubleshooting, opening new areas, serving as Regional Vice President, and handling Home Pac sales. Home Pacs was a separate division of Pepe's Pizza—and it involved a network of men, women, and children doing part-time work delivering to their friends and neighbors everything needed in a box to make their own pizzas in their home. These were good years when I learned much that has helped me throughout my life.

We wanted only partners who wanted our products and those who would be blessed with our products and service.

Those learnings included being transparent with those we do business with and not putting pressure on people to buy—but at the same time not accepting the first, second, third, or even fourth no. When a salesman knows something is "good" for a person or business, he can persist by showing love, sincerity, and empathy.

We wanted only partners who wanted our products and those who would be blessed with our products and service.

I learned that persistence is the key to success. I can identify with what the great American inventor Thomas Edison once said: "Genius is 1% inspiration and 99% perspiration."

– 9 –

A Life-Changing Accident

January 2010

As I sit here at a perfectly crafted Italian desk looking out through six-foot French doors, I am in awe. Venice, Italy, is as beautiful in January as it is in late October. Right outside my window is the Grand Canal. Every kind of boat is before me. Wholesale food companies are delivering needed products to restaurants and hotels using boats that hold as much material as our 17-foot pizza trucks. Trash is being picked up by similar boats. People are milling about, walking and catching boats to other islands. There are skilled artists painting and selling their colorful artwork. People are sitting at comfortable outside tables enjoying local vino, espressos, cold drinks, and wonderful Italian food. There are Africans standing in front of their leather goods, offering them for sale. Boat taxis are busy running people to Murano. Gondolas are taking their passengers through the canals, and you can hear the guides singing joyous Italian songs. Across the canal is Lido Beach, where I intend to go today.

> As I slept last night, my thoughts turned to Cheryl and how very special she is and was to me. Warm and loving—and always happy and enthusiastic about life. I was so fortunate to have loved Cheryl and to have experienced her love during our 38 years. As I now think about her and how truly precious she is, I thank God for her and our children. I thank God for the spouses of my children and my grandchildren. I thank God for all the people who have worked with us through the years. I thank God for my three brothers and three younger sisters, my parents, and Cheryl's parents and brothers and sisters. I thank God for my uncles and aunts, who certainly prayed for us. I thank God for my nephews and nieces. Finally, I thank God for what He taught me in the mid-1980s back in Kentucky.

One dark, cold, rainy night about 1984 in eastern Kentucky, with over two hours left before I would get back home, something happened that changed my life. I was driving out of Sadieville around 11 p.m. in my pizza service van, going at least 65 miles an hour. I ran a stop sign, crossed a busy two-lane road where coal trucks are usually active, jumped a ditch, and ended up on the side of a muddy hill. (Over the years when traveling to many areas of the country, I would at times forget exactly where I was. I might think I was in southern

Indiana when I was in South Carolina. When you travel to different places each week, your mind doesn't always keep up with where you are. This is common when people travel a lot. Sixteen hours on the road can do this to you also! In this case I ran a stop sign because I had forgotten I was not on a highway. The stop sign just came up on me unexpectedly.) My van was stuck in the mud and couldn't move up or down. I would have to step out and walk in the mud to get a tow truck. (There were no cell phones at this time.) As I sat there, I asked God what He wanted me to do and what was going on. The van was a new one I had owned for just two months.

[Two months earlier, I had totaled my previous van trying to pull it back onto the road after my right wheels dropped onto the shoulder at normal highway speed. Instead of returning to the road, the van swung hard to the left, crossed the highway, and hit the side of a mountain with its front end. It did the same with its back end, and finally turned over and slid to a stop. The van was totaled, but I wasn't scratched. The first vehicle that came around the curve was a pickup truck driven by a businessman. He stopped and helped me transfer everything from my van to his truck, then drove me the 100 miles to my warehouse, which meant he wouldn't get back to his home until after 1 a.m. He became a customer and a good friend.]

As I sat there ... seeking a word from God and feeling very low, I heard the Holy Spirit tell me, in my spirit, to run my business as though I were in a wheelchair.

As I sat there on that muddy hill outside Sadieville seeking a word from God and feeling very low, I heard the Holy Spirit tell me, in my spirit, to run my business as though I were in a wheelchair. I made a decision then and there that I would hire others to do most of the driving and servicing so I would need to spend less time on the road. I then noticed that the front porch light of a nearby home had been turned on. A man was walking toward me from the home. He yelled to me that he had phoned for a tow truck. It wasn't long before the truck pulled me down and got me back on the road. I never did step out of the van into the mud. No damage to the van or me, but God had gotten my attention. You see, I had driven many miles through 20 states while helping develop Pepe's Pizza and now building my own company. I agreed with the Holy Spirit that evening that I needed to operate my business as though I were in a wheelchair.

Because I listened to the Holy Spirit and began running my business as from a wheelchair, I hired people to help me do what had to be done. I had to trust others with the responsibilities of leadership and carrying out my vision. A person in a wheelchair must depend on a team. God sent me men and women who took ownership of their positions. We grew exponentially in all directions. It was a business built on trust and good ethics.

God led me to put everyone in the company on a base pay plus commission. Everyone had the opportunity to earn as much as he or she needed or wanted, based on the sales under their responsibility. Office and warehouse personnel also earned their commissions based on the sales of the company.

Because of this model, employees motivated each other to increase sales. My personal income grew, as did the income of our people.

The most important people are the ones on the front line. The men and women who are facing customers daily must take ownership and be given the authority to make decisions on the spot at times. Most companies could get along with less management by giving their front-line people more power to make decisions, motivating them to take more ownership of their responsibilities.

December 2009

> It's not good for man to be alone. As I walk the streets of Venice and see the happy couples and see their love for each other, I pray to God that He will send me a lady who loves me as Cheryl did. I have surrendered this to the Master and Creator of all that is. I have told God that I will not seek or pursue a woman. If He wants me to have another lady in my life, He will have to make it happen. I shared with Him the other evening how much I need the warmth of a woman, the smell and feel of a woman in my life. I would only want a woman who truly loves me as I am, who is happy and full of life.

She would have to be a lady who enjoys traveling and walking and visiting places out of the way. A woman who loves my children and grandchildren.

The following paragraph is from God's Word: Luke 21:34–36. [The emphasis is mine.]

> *Be careful, or your hearts will be weighed down with dissipation, drunkenness, and the anxieties of life, and that day will close on you unexpectedly like a trap. For it will come upon all those who live on the face of the whole earth. Be always on the watch, and pray that you may be able to escape all that is about to happen, and that you may be able to* stand before the Son of Man.

You see, God does not put us in *hell.* We choose by our deeds whether we can *stand before the Son of God.* Our God has given us *His* Son in place of our sins so that we can stand up before our God. Though we are saved by the stripes of Jesus, can we *stand before the Son of God on that day?*

Today I am sitting in Siena, Italy, in a most beautiful, quaint hotel by the name of Campo Regio Relais. I am looking out at a hill covered from the bottom to the top with homes, narrow streets, shops, and, at the very summit of Siena, the largest cathedral in the city—Duomo di Siena. The cathedral is so large there is continuous repair work to keep it in good condition. I was told that as soon as they finish repairing it, they start over. It was built more than 900 years ago. Siena is a city built by the Romans within tall walls for its protection. It is very hilly, even more so than San Francisco. One of the most interesting things a visitor will notice is the physical stamina of the people walking the streets. People of all ages walking as fast as they can up and down hills that most people in America would not consider walking. Women and men in their late years, many stooped over, walking steadily up and down steep hills that had me gasping for breath.

Yes, I am so fortunate to be able to visit Italy again for these three weeks. Traveling here by myself has made this trip somewhat of a retreat. The beautiful places I stay in and the things I see make me miss Cheryl even more. Cheryl was a good traveling companion. She was always happy wherever we stayed. She was full of joy—joy from the Lord.

The question arises: Would I want to live in Europe? As I ponder that thought the answer comes to me: only if I found that special woman who loved me for myself. Europe or any place is nice to visit, but without the ones you love it becomes lonely. I find myself looking into the eyes of the women I meet. What does that mean? I think it means that I need companionship, and yet I have surrendered that need to God. At my age of 69, I have had a full life. Over 38 years with a woman who loved me and whom I loved. God has blessed me with eight healthy children who are all special and independent in their thinking. All of

> them are competent to carry on after my passing. Our business is healthy and will be carried on by the present management and some of the children. My brothers, sisters, nephews, and nieces will always be ready to mentor them as needed.

2011

Let me speak of the principles I pray my children will adhere to throughout their lives. I must say that I believe our children already follow most of the principles set down by Cheryl and me.

In order to love others, you must love yourself. How do you love yourself? I can speak only from my own experience. I have peace and joy—and, yes, I love myself—when I am in God's will. Indeed, I know Jesus died for my sins and I am forgiven of all my sins. But even though this is true, when I sin I lose peace and joy, and I don't love myself or the ones around me. Throughout my life's journey I've learned that real peace and joy, the bubbling-out joy, comes when I am in God's will. Every decision not to sin helps me grow the right habits. God honors the desires of our hearts, and He knows my true desire is to always stay in His will. Jesus' death for our sins—past, present, and future—doesn't mean we Christians can sin as we like. A habitual pattern of sinning can take us away from our salvation. Life is full of choices, and real joy is when we make the right choices. It is the deepest intent of our heart that matters to God. Remember what God said to Samuel when he was at Jesse's house (before David the shepherd boy was summoned from the field)? *"Man looks at the outward appearance, but the Lord looks at the heart"* (1 Samuel 16:7). We don't want to do anything that is wrong in God's eyes because we want the joy that can be known through being in God's will. I believe this is what God honors and what Jesus died for.

When I do something unexpected for someone else to show my love, then I have joy. It may be giving a larger-than-normal tip for service or anonymously paying for the meal of someone at the next table. Whatever makes for the "magic moment." It's a seed planted toward a harvest, however God wants it to grow. I receive joy and peace when I give of myself or offer financial help when needed. If you haven't read the book *Moments of Magic* by Shep Hyken, I would encourage you to do so. It speaks of extraordinary things that happen on some days because someone does something that is such a special, out-of-the-ordinary blessing. Someone goes out of his or her way to make a difference in another's life, doing something no one would have expected, creating a magic moment. I look for these magic moments with anticipation, wonderment, and appreciation. When such moments happen to me, they create the opportunity for me to spontaneously reciprocate with a magic moment of my own for that individual.

– 10 –

The Essence of Life

I wrote the following while sitting in the Grand Hotel Excelsior Vittoria in Sorrento, Italy. As I looked out the window over the Bay of Naples at Mount Vesuvius, I decided to begin explaining my life and my personal principles in hopes that they may be of some help to my readers.

2010

Certainly the essence of life includes staying in good physical health so that I will live a healthy life and be able to enjoy my children's children's children (as a great-grandpa!). It for sure included loving Cheryl through a long, wonderful life. Helping others know the Good News that Jesus died on the cross for our sins and that, if we believe He did so, we will have eternal life. Raising our children to know Jesus and have healthy attitudes about life, money, and responsibility. Providing my family with finances for education without having borrowed money to do so. Building a home for my family that is comfortable and safe. Having someday written a book, or books, if I have something to say that is of value.

It is true that love is a "many-splendored thing." Jesus said the greatest commandment is twofold: to love God and to love one's neighbor as oneself. This is so true, and adherence to these precepts is greatly needed by all of us. We need to be loved and to love. Jesus died on the cross because He loves us and wants us with Him for eternity. God is love. It is so important to thank Jesus all through the day for this love.

The most practical and known way is to give of ourselves to help others; if we do so, we will find love.

A life without love is boring and lonely. Yet no one has to stay in the desert and be without water. There is a way to leave the lonely place and find love. The most practical and known way is to give of ourselves to help others; if we do so, we will find love. We will receive so much more back than we give. There are many ways all around us to volunteer to help others. People who give some time to help others are happy and develop many wonderful new friends. The essence of life includes planting seeds—using money and using ourselves. This is accomplished through family and everyone we meet each day. We should never take love for granted, as it moves away so easily if not nurtured. How do we nurture love? In my experience it is an ongoing process. We show our love in words of love and actions of love throughout each day. We show our love by the little things we do for others without looking for a reward. We show our love by listening, really listening. We show our love by truly showing interest in what is said, even when we feel we don't have time or interest.

A wonderful example of love was my mother's love. My mother was so precious. With four boys and three girls she was what love was truly meant to be. Matilda was her name, and her brothers and sisters called her Tillie. She's in heaven surely preparing wonderful meals for all who sit at her table. She was kind, thoughtful, patient, caring, loving, inspiring, courageous, strong, humble, happy, not judgmental, a good listener, and always a friend. Mother lived 87 years and always seemed happy and vibrant. When she passed on to heaven it was like a whisper; she just went back to sleep.

All the riches you can accumulate are of no value without love, so don't go another day without love. Find a place where you can give some of your time to help others. No matter what age you are. You may be a young person who can't seem to meet a young man or woman, and you are lonely. Volunteer some of your time to help others, and you will plant a seed toward finding that person. If you are a bored or lonely senior, find a place where you have an interest and where you can give some of your time to help others, and you will find love.

God is so good to His children. He has put certain principles in place on this earth. "Seedtime and harvest" is one of them. Plant a seed, and you get a harvest. From just one tomato seed many tomatoes and a multitude of seeds are harvested! The principle of seedtime and harvest appears in every facet of our world. If you want love, you must give love! God gave His Son to die for us, and the harvest of this love is in the millions who will have eternal life. That's the Good News. The harvest is free! The seed, Jesus, has been planted; all you have to do is believe this, and you can have eternal life.

Everything on earth starts with a seed. Give, and it will be given to you. Love, and you will find love. Volunteer, and you will reap a harvest of love. Develop the spirit of giving.

– 11 –

Seedtime and Harvest

Remember this: Whoever sows sparingly will also reap sparingly, and whoever sows generously will also reap generously. Each man should give what he has decided in his heart to give, not reluctantly or under compulsion, for God loves a cheerful giver. And God is able to make all grace abound to you, so that in all things at all times, having all that you need, you will abound in every good work. As it is written:

"He has scattered abroad his gifts to the poor; his righteousness endures forever."

Now he who supplies seed to the sower and bread for food will also supply and increase your store of seed and will enlarge the harvest of your righteousness.

—2 Corinthians 9:6–10

Throughout my Christian life God has put it on my heart to share with those in need. There were three occasions before I became a Christian when people asked me to loan them

> *If I give money, I give it in the name of Jesus and say it's a gift—and add that someday the person might be able to help someone else.*

money. They quoted terms and wanted to pay me interest and told me exactly how they would pay me back. Being the kindhearted person I am, with sincere empathy I loaned them the money. At times the money I loaned was from my savings. Money I needed and wanted returned to me. I was never paid back. Instead of paying me back, my debtors ignored their debts and messed up our relationship. Loaning money to a friend has become a no-brainer: It ruins friendships. It took those three occasions before I learned this lesson.

After I realized these people had no intention of paying me back, because they never mentioned the debt or attempted to repay me, I wrote them a letter telling them I did not want them to pay me back, to consider the money a gift. Now why did I do this? Because the money they had borrowed was on my mind every time I saw them, and sometimes when I didn't see them. I would wonder why they were spending money on beer or cigarettes when they owed me money. I was brought up to value the dollar and taught that if someone loaned me something it should be repaid as agreed. I didn't want to live with the feeling I had toward these people. Once I forgave the debt, I had peace and didn't worry about it again.

Because of this lesson, I don't loan money to anyone. If anyone asks me for money, I seek guidance from God as to whether I should help the person. If I give money, I give it in the name of Jesus and say it's a gift—and add that someday the person might be able to help someone else. Normally when someone asks me for money, the person asks for a specific amount. After praying about the matter, I usually give the individual a little more than he or she asked for. We can't outgive God, and this kind of giving is another opportunity to plant a seed for a harvest.

> *Command them to do good, to be rich in good deeds, and to be generous and willing to share. In this way they will*

lay up treasure for themselves as a firm foundation for the coming age, so that they may take hold of the life that is truly life.

—1 Timothy 6:18–19

It's all about seedtime and harvest. Everything on earth starts with a seed, and from that seed, no matter how small it is, come many seeds and new life.

The Hunt family company Seedtime & Harvest was so named in order to continually remind us to give to others if we expect a harvest. The more seed we plant in God's name, the more of a blessing we can be to others. A worthy goal is a budget that enables us to live on what we've socked away and to devote 100% of our income to helping others. There was a time in my life when I asked homeless people who stopped me to request money why they wouldn't get a job and work for their money like the rest of us. One day it dawned on me that it really didn't matter if they used money given to them to buy more wine or drugs. I should give as they asked and tell them I was doing so in the name of Jesus. The name Jesus is so powerful; it changes lives. As a result of this approach, a person who may not have thought about God for years may, through me, hear the name Jesus spoken. Jesus may enter the person's thinking and heart just through the speaking of the name Jesus. Even if the person spends the money given to him or her foolishly, I will still have planted a seed for a future harvest.

> *When we are generous with what we have, God is generous with us. A life of giving with open hands is a wonderful life.*

I do believe a harvest can come in many different ways. Your harvest may not be in money. Many times I have planted a seed and told God I was doing so toward a major business decision or toward a need of one of my children. When we are generous with what we have, God is generous with us. A life of giving with open hands is a wonderful life. Just like George Bailey's experience in the movie *It's a Wonderful Life*.

One day I ordered food at a drive-in fast-food franchise. When I drove up to pick up the food and pay, the cashier told me the driver of the car ahead of me had paid for my order. When I learned this, the person had already driven off, so I couldn't say thanks. I don't believe the person knew me, and I didn't look like I needed someone to buy my lunch. The driver just decided to do a "random act of kindness" for the next patron. A seed was planted; it was a magic moment (see Chapter 9) for both of us. I learned from this and have often now done the same for others.

On another occasion, my family and I went to a pizza restaurant, and we needed another table to pull up next to the one we were given. A young couple was eating at the table next to ours, and that table was the one needed. The young man offered to move to another table without us asking. I later told the waiter to give me their bill—that I wanted to pay for their meal. I'm sure that the young man's generous offer to move was as much of a *magic moment* for him and his wife as it was for us. When I have seen others dining out for whom I thought money could be a problem, I have paid their bills and done so without them knowing who did it. This is planting seeds for a harvest.

The amount of soliciting we receive by mail is completely out of hand, so I give only to organizations that I personally know are doing God's work and using money wisely. I prefer to give locally when possible. Tipping waitresses and waiters is important to me. Since my father was a restaurant owner and we children worked in the business, we know how exhausting the restaurant business can be. I also know that many restaurant employees don't always earn enough to live on. Many waitresses are single mothers having a rough time making ends meet. If service is good, I tip extra well. If service is excellent, I tip even better than extra well.

At the age of 65 I started to receive Social Security checks. I never believed I should be given this money since there are so many others who need it more than I do. Since the U.S. Social Security program is having financial problems, I wonder why the government doesn't give everyone who earns above a certain amount, or whose assets total so much in value, the option not to receive Social Security checks. Somewhere along the line I decided to give my monthly Social Security dollars to people each month as I saw need. This decision has been a blessing to me and has certainly resulted in magic moments for a number of recipients.

– 12 –

Open Your Hands

Are your hands closed tightly into a fist? Look at your hands and close them into a tight fist. Now open them up and hold them in front of you and look at them. Do you see and feel the difference? Do you notice how beautiful and relaxed they are when they are opened up? It's like the difference between night and day when you open them up.

Why so beautiful? Because I believe open hands are a sign of surrender, love, giving and receiving, humbleness, submission, openness, and praise.

Giving to others is so important for each of us throughout our lives. Not holding on tightly to what we have, but sharing whatever we have with others. Giving is among the most important principles for success in life, second only perhaps to love.

> *As we make a fist and hold on to all we have, we turn inward. When we turn inward, we lose something that we need: love for others.*

As we make a fist and hold on to all we have, we turn inward. When we turn inward, we lose something that we need: love for others. We must turn outward, look at the needs of those around us, and be open-handed to help those who have needs. My experience has shown, as I noted earlier, that we can't outgive God. The more seed we plant by helping others, the greater our harvest will be in all areas of our lives. Again, as Paul wrote to the Corinthians:

> *You will be made rich in every way so that you can be generous on every occasion, and … your generosity will result in thanksgiving to God.*
>
> *This service that you perform is not only supplying the needs of God's people but is also overflowing in many expressions of thanks to God. Because of the service by which you have proved yourselves, men will praise God*

for the obedience that accompanies your confession of the gospel of Christ, and for your generosity in sharing with them and with everyone else. And in their prayers for you their hearts will go out to you, because of the surpassing grace God has given you. Thanks be to God for his indescribable gift!

—2 Corinthians 9:11–15

Richard Foster in *Money, Sex and Power* says, "Just the very act of letting go of money, or some other treasure, does something within us. It destroys the demon greed."

As a businessman for nearly 50 years, I've been privileged to be able to provide financial and prayer support for a number of Christian ministries. One that has been especially close to my heart the past decade is African Projects for Peace and Love Initiatives.

In 2002 our daughter Rachel started attending Oral Roberts University in Tulsa, Oklahoma. Cheryl and I drove her to school to help her get settled in. While we were there, Cheryl and I decided to go up into the Prayer Tower and pray for Rachel's success and for God's protection on her life while in college. We were directed into one of the prayer rooms, and there right before us was this man on his knees wearing a suit and tie without his shoes, praising God aloud. This is how I met Titus K. Oyeyemi from Lagos, Nigeria. That very day God put it on my heart to support his God-given mission to pursue peace in every area of human life—and to create in his students the desire and education to bring about a true renaissance in Africa, the Future Land of Peace.

In March 2010 Rachel and I visited Titus and his wife, Fehintola, in Lagos, and we saw for ourselves the impact of what God is doing through Titus and his vision for peace (see three photos prior to Chapter 17).

– 13 –

Money: What's It For?

Money is used to exchange or trade goods with others. At this time in the history of the United States, we use the dollar. Our dollar's value differs from that of other countries' units of currency. The American dollar is worth more than some countries' units of currency—and worth less than other countries' units of currency.

Bartering, a manner of trading goods with others that predates the advent of money, is still a way of life for many. Actually, this is how exchange and trade began. One person needed salt and the other needed sweet potatoes, so they agreed to a swap based on their needs. That is pretty much what many still do today: "I'll give you this amount in exchange for that something." As young boys growing up, we brothers and our neighborhood buddies would swap, or trade, comic books and marbles. We did this continually. We would go to a friend's house and knock on the door, and Bobby's mother would yell, "Jimmy is here to trade!" Bobby would come bounding down the stairs with a stack of Marvel comic books, ready to barter.

Many times wealth is the result of just being in the right place at the right time and having the initiative to take advantage of the opportunity.

The American Indians traded furs for beads, firearms, and many other things they wanted from the white man. Tiger paws, wild boar meat, crocodile hides, and the skins of many other animals also have been valuable trading items used for bartering in different parts of the world.

Some people are able to accumulate more wealth than others through hard work and good decisions. Many times wealth is the result of just being in the right place at the right time and having the initiative to take advantage of the opportunity. Still others become wealthy through inheritance. Many good people have a financially hard life and never seem to meet their material needs. There are very contented people in both of these positions of life. The wise have a good attitude no matter what their financial situation. There are those who aren't happy even though they're wealthy. There also are those who have very little and cannot accept their position; they do things to ruin their lives and the lives of those they love. And I've known families that were happy without much money.

Money is not the key to happiness. Whether money is earned or inherited makes no difference, so long as we have the right perspective. I believe we should leave an inheritance to our children and our children's children. An inheritance can be the wisdom to live a good life, one of integrity, with love for one's fellow man. If an inheritance is of financial wealth, then the beneficiary is urged to be thankful and use it wisely. If we plant good seeds, the wealth we are left with, in whatever form, will grow so that we can leave our children an inheritance.

The Marriott hotels, in public estimation, are among the most superior in the world. J. W. Marriott got his start in the restaurant business. He featured root beer and called his company Hot Shoppes. He then moved into the hotel business. Before he died he turned the business over to his son J. W. Marriott Jr., who took his inheritance and developed the Marriott chain into one of the world's finest, thereby multiplying the inheritance he had received ten thousand–fold.

This is how a person who receives an inheritance is encouraged to see his good fortune. An inheritance truly is a blessing that is to be appreciated, shared, and grown for the next generation. It is true, however, that this viewpoint is not shared by all. I have observed that most people fortunate to receive an inheritance don't pass it on but instead, through poor business judgment, lack of wisdom, or poor advice, lose most if not all of it.

Bottom line: Money is a tool—no more, no less.

Bottom line: Money is a tool—no more, no

less. When one needs a tool such as a knife, one knows how important it is to have it. Money has the same importance; it is much better to have money than not to have it. When we have money we can take it for granted and spend it foolishly—and one day find we are short of it. It's like having a bag of M&M's or a nice, thick milkshake. Coming to the end of it and realizing it's gone, we wish we had gone through it more slowly. A line from a '60s song comes to mind: "Don't it always seem to go that you don't know what you got till it's gone." Money can be spent foolishly and slip through our fingers so quickly—money that was earned and accumulated over many years of hard work and through conservative spending and investment. There are few free lunches in the financial world. The majority of people who have accumulated large sums of money and left an inheritance worked at their profession every day. They had a savings plan and often shared with those in need. They lived within their income and lived debt-free. Even as their wealth grew, they continued to live conservatively.

A dollar saved is a dollar earned. That's why being debt-free is so important. A house mortgage paid out over 15 or 30 years could mean paying more than $200,000 or $300,000 in interest. You must pray for wisdom in administering your finances. Also make use of trustworthy counsel, found through quality references.

Don't tie your self-worth to your money. As I mentioned, money is a tool, but just like any tool, such as a lawn mower, its permanency is not guaranteed; it will rust and be gone if not cared for. Read the Bible for wisdom in all your financial decision making. This one book is the cornerstone, the financial foundation, of what is needed; it is the Word of the God who owns it all and who says, *"Ask and you will receive"* (Matthew 7:7). Put your faith in His Word. Also as I noted earlier, real wisdom in this world comes through STP: surrender, trust, and praising God daily.

My wife, Cheryl, our children (we had five at the time), and I once experienced a few days with the extended Hunt family at my brother Lonnie's log cabin on the Ohio River in Kentucky, a wonderful, rustic, comfortable cabin that Lonnie had built from the trees in that area. It had a wraparound balcony and was constructed 10 feet above the ground, in case the Ohio

River flooded. Inside the cabin was a small balcony looking down at a massive, four-foot-stone fireplace. There was no running water. Instead Lonnie had a cistern and a pump by the sink to bring in water. Outside, in full view of the river, he had built an outhouse just like the one in the Li'l Abner comic strip. It leaned to one side somewhat, but it had a smooth, wooden toilet seat that was surprisingly comfortable. The door didn't stay closed too well, but we didn't care. We loved that cabin getaway.

There was a potbelly wood-burning stove known to have served the finest fried chicken, mashed potatoes and gravy, green beans, and homemade biscuits my brother Lonnie could muster. In the morning, we had hot, strong coffee with beignets and bacon. Lonnie has always enjoyed cooking; he certainly whipped up some good vittles at that cabin. That was good eatin'! Even though we ate by candlelight in temperatures below freezing, we felt we were in heaven. My brothers and I would sit up most of the night in front of a roaring fire discussing everything that could be talked about. There were nights when we cooked our steaks and potatoes to perfection in the fireplace. These are good memories that I assure you have rekindled a strong desire in me for steak and potatoes roasted in a fireplace. I guarantee you it will happen very soon.

One night after the others had returned home, it was just Cheryl, the children, and I. As we sat by the fireplace following a delicious dinner, my precious Cheryl entertained our five children and me with a story. The only light we had was from candles and the fireplace. Our dog, a beautiful, white Samoyed named Tasha, lay at our feet. I would like to share Cheryl's story with you. Cheryl was a gifted storyteller, and this (as I recall it) was her story for our children. I believe it speaks to all of us.

> A woodcutter named Lucas told his wife, Emma, "I wait and I wait, and I know the good Lord will see to it that we will be blessed many, many times. I only thank Him every day for our children and for our soup and for the wood that I bring in to these people in the villages. I thank God for the helping hands in the wintertime, getting this wood out of the cold and into the people's warm firerooms. I don't complain, Emma; you love me and you've lived with me a long time."
>
> "Oh Lucas," Emma said. "Make more money or I'll leave."

Finally, after many months of bickering and yelling, Lucas said, "Well, Lord, maybe I need to listen to Emma."

So the very next morning Lucas set out for the large, large city where there were many worlds, many people working very hard for their money. They lived on high mountaintops in beautiful mansions, mansions that were filled with the most beautiful furniture and the finest furs and diamonds. The children went to the best schools and turned out to be the finest lawyers and doctors.

Lucas looked at all of this and said, "Maybe this is for me." He was gone one month and then two months and then three months, and it ran into six months. After six months and very little good fortune, he became downhearted to the point that he thought God was turning His back on him, and his wife was definitely going to leave him. So he prayed a special prayer that night: "Oh God, I listen to you and I listen to my wife. What should I hear? What voice should I hear? Is it yours that is right, and is it yours that I'm hearing, or is it my wife's that is right? Do I have to really, really work hard and do without helping people and strive to be a rich man?"

That very night he dreamed very, very long dreams that he had never dreamed in his whole life. He dreamed of his children as they grew and entered into their lives with their wonderful families. In his final dream he met a little man along a pathway in the snow. He woke up the next morning, then he went out into the world determined to make a lot of money to be rich so Emma would be happy, and maybe he would be happy too.

As Lucas was walking along, a little man came by, just as in the dream. The little man carried a small, white bag, which was hanging out of his pocket. The little man didn't give his name, but Lucas knew that he was someone special because he had dreamed of him. He knew something had happened with his prayer to God. The little man invited Lucas to his home to visit his family and his children. Lucas entered into the beautiful world he had been trying to get into for the longest time.

The little man was very rich. He sat in the largest chair in his home. It was his chair that was set aside just for him. He sat there, and he said to Lucas, "An angel has sent me to you, and I know in my heart that what I have to tell you is going to mean very much to you." He reached into his pocket and pulled out the small, white bag—and what do you think was in that bag? Five copper pennies.

In the man's beautiful home there was a lovely fire burning in the fireplace, and the little man said, "Lucas, this first night that you are in my home I am going to toss into the fire the first copper penny, and you will see what will happen." So Lucas listened and agreed; he thought the coin was being tossed because of the prayer he had prayed. So the man went ahead and tossed the penny into the fire, and the beautiful fire flamed up high and turned many beautiful colors.

The next morning Lucas, as he had been doing for the last few months, set out to work at his job in the city. He was very successful on this day. He sold his goods for twice the amount of money he had paid for them in the first place. People were buying from him; they were buying left and right. Walking along he met the little man again, and he invited Lucas to his home again. Lucas went to the man's home and had a fine dinner with the whole family. After everyone else had gone to bed, the little man tossed another penny into the fire.

The next morning, as he was walking along trying to make more money for Emma, Lucas met a horse and carriage, and in the carriage was a very small lamb. It was alone and it was crying; he knew that he had to take care of the lamb. He carefully picked up the beautiful, white lamb and carried that lamb into every town he walked to that day. People wanted to buy the lamb from Lucas because it was very white and very young and pretty, but he knew he had to keep the lamb.

That evening he met the little man again, and the man tossed the third penny into the fire. He said, "Tomorrow, since I have thrown the third penny into the fire, Lucas, you will see beautiful things happen to you."

Lucas said, "How much more beautiful can they be? So far I have had so many good things happening to me."

The little man said, "Just go on your way and you will see."

The next morning, after Lucas awakened, he carried his lamb in his wagon, and after traveling awhile he came across an old road that had not been used in many, many years. While on that road he encountered a horse and a cow that belonged to an old woman who had been working very hard for many years to serve her family. Her husband had died, and she was supporting her children and taking care of them. "Good morning," Lucas said. "I've got a lamb; you've got a horse and a cow. Could we work together?" The old woman agreed and joined Lucas with her horse and her cow. They then walked on and went from town to town using their animals for many good things to help people and also to earn money. They carried the little lamb everywhere they went. They shared their work and were very happy.

This went on for a couple of weeks and then a few more weeks past that. The lamb grew and was very, very large and was now a beautiful, white sheep. Lucas then purchased a daddy sheep to keep his beautiful, white sheep company, with the thought that it would be a good way to earn more money in the future. The very evening he bought the daddy sheep, he met the little man again. He hadn't seen him for several months, and the man invited Lucas to his fine home and served him a very delicious dinner. That evening he tossed the fourth penny into the fire. Even more brilliant colors shone from the fire after the man tossed the fourth penny in, which meant something even more amazing was going to happen. Lucas was so excited he could hardly sleep; he tossed and turned all night because he just couldn't wait to see what would happen the next day.

The very next morning Lucas met up with the old woman, her cow, and her horse, along with his mother and father sheep. The day was good because they helped people who couldn't pay for their services, as well as those who could; they had a very profitable day. And then one morning Lucas woke up to the bleating of two of the cutest little baby lambs he had ever seen. In the days following the birth of the baby lambs, it was evident that the mommy sheep was giving much more milk than the baby lambs needed, too much for those babies. So, Lucas was able to sell the fresh sheep's milk, which was a delicacy in that area. People really went for that sheep's milk. More baby lambs were born over time, so the animals grew in number. The cow also was giving milk, and the horse gave children rides, which their parents paid for. There was lots of milk to sell, and Lucas and the old woman were getting rich.

All of this was happening so quickly it seemed like a miracle. While out selling the milk one day, Lucas came across the little man, who said, "Please come to my home for dinner, and we will see what the fifth penny will do for you."

Lucas said, "Oh, I feel so bad that I've never done anything for you. What can I do for you sometime?"

The little man answered, "Let's not think about what you can do for me. Let me show you what else the Lord has for you."

So Lucas went to the man's home for dinner, and the fifth penny was thrown into the fire. The fire grew very large and then ... very small.

The very next morning Lucas went on to his work, and there was a great, great storm that came into town. The storm blew many buildings down. People lost their homes. It was so terrible. People were crying and sad. Children were wandering in the road of the village. Lucas and the old woman didn't know what they could do. But they knew they had to do something. So they went to work. The horse and was put to work pulling a big wagon carrying a lot of things from burnt-down homes that had caught on fire after the storm. The children were taken out of the storm area to a safe place. Milk from the sheep and the cow was served to the children, one after the other, until all were full and happy.

Then Lucas thought to himself, *It's time to go home to Emma.* He had made a lot of money, and he had a lot of money saved, from this beautiful, beautiful gift God had given to him. The Lord had let him go into business with the old woman and share in all the money they earned. The horse, the cow, the sheep, and the lambs were such a blessing. He was so thankful for all this that had happened in his life, and Lucas was anxious to go home to his wife and family to tell them how good God is to His children. But one thing he wondered about was that because the fire had dropped down low after the fifth penny was thrown in, it might mean everything could be taken away from him.

Emma was so surprised to see Lucas return home. He had been gone a long time. Emma looked much older to Lucas. She had aged over the time he had been away. Lucas didn't want to see her that way. He said, "Emma, I'll never go away from you again, but what I do have to tell you is that we now have much money."

Emma cried and cried. She broke down at the table after the fine meal she had given him, and she said, "Oh Lucas, you've been gone so many months; so many things have happened to me. I began going to church again after you left. I missed you so much, and I knew God had something for me while you were gone. He told me we could have a million diamonds stowed away, we could have coins packed in giant boxes stored in the attic, and all these riches could be ours, but they wouldn't mean anything if I constantly yelled and screamed at you for not going out to get me money. You were happy in the first place with your humble life. The money wasn't worth my loneliness and the children's loneliness at all. I'm sorry that I made you leave and be gone for all these months."

Lucas was saddened by Emma's tears, but he was happy for her new life. They knew they were rich because of the trust they had in God and because they still loved each other, even after all the hard times they had been through. Now Emma appreciated Lucas, rich or poor. She was a happy woman. Their friends visited them often in their beautiful home, and they lived happily ever after. They thanked God every day both for their poor life and for their rich life. When Lucas and Emma and their children went to bed, they thanked God most of all for the wonderful gift of life itself.

And that's the end of the story!

– 14 –

What Values Are Important in Life?

To answer this question I must rephrase it by asking myself, *What has been important or valuable to me in my life?*

- My faith that Jesus is who He says He is and that all He said while on this earth is true.
- My belief that the Bible is the inspired Word of God.
- The Good News is that because of Jesus, our Savior and Lord, we will not just die and rot, but our spirits will rise and live for eternity.
- My dear wife, Cheryl, our sons and daughters, their husbands and wives, and our grandchildren.
- Unchanging values that America must get back to—basic values that made America a great country.

- Respect for others' talents and abilities.
- Respect for women as mothers, daughters, or wives.
- Men's respect for their wives; the cherishing of the love of their youth.
- Husbands' complete family support, such that wives don't need to find work outside the home—unless that is their heart's desire.
- Men's pursuit of moral integrity and taking on responsibility for their families.
- Honor of father and mother.
- The realization that today's actions will be our future's memories. What kind of memories will we have?
- The realization that love is the world's greatest need: loving God and loving our neighbors as ourselves.
- Saying what we mean and meaning what we say.
- A word or handshake that is as good as a formal, written contract.
- Sharing of whatever we have with those in need.
- Family prayer in the home.
- Growing in faith by reading the Word of God.

- Standing up for our beliefs.
- Standing up against immoral businesses in our cities.
- Teaching our children strong morals.
- Taking responsibility for our debts.
- Speaking out against injustice.
- Getting rid of the attitude that we deserve something for nothing.
- The realization that abortion is the murder of a living human being.
- Teaching our children in our homes the importance of moral sexuality.
- An urgent call that the Ten Commandments be displayed in our public schools and government buildings.
- The importance of the United States allowing prayer in our public schools.
- The freedom as Americans to preach from the rooftops, "United we stand!" and "In God we trust!"
- The realization that marriage was meant to be between a man and a woman, just as God made the animal also to reproduce with the opposite sex. It is abnormal for two

males or two females to engage in sexual activity with one another. Such abnormality has never been accepted at any time by a society without dire consequences. Greece and Rome are examples, Sodom and Gomorrah another. Is America heading down a similar road?

– 15 –

Faith and Trust as a Child

2009

When I put fuel in a car, truck, boat, lawnmower, or tractor, I have faith that it will move that piece of equipment. When I flip a light switch, I have faith that the light will come on. When I put food in a freezer, I have faith that it will freeze. We usually have faith in our leaders and at times may be willing to follow them into battle or toward a new business goal. As children, we jump off a wall into the arms of our father without any fear because we have faith that Dad will catch us. I don't have "faith questions" in these matters. Yet, as children of God, all too often we have trouble with *religious* faith. We are more like "doubting" Thomas and need to put our fingers in Jesus' side and see where the spear pierced him and see his hands still showing the scars from the nails.

How do we find faith in our heavenly Father? We get that kind of faith through reading the Word of God daily and by praying. Praying that the Holy Spirit will increase our faith and give us faith like a child's. Trust God, trust His Word, and live a life of faith.

Recently in my readings I came across a story about two travelers whose flight was becoming pretty rough. They were bouncing around in the sky. One man was reading the Bible, and as the flight became increasingly scary, the other man said, "You don't actually believe that Bible stuff, do you?"

Looking up from his reading, the first man replied, "Yes, I do."

"Well, do you believe how that guy Jonah was swallowed by a whale and lived to tell about it?"

"Oh yeah, I believe he was swallowed—and the whale spit him out on dry land."

"How could a person survive something like that?"

The first man answered, "That's a good question; when I get to heaven, I just might look up ol' Jonah and ask him."

"Well," harrumphed the other man, "what if Jonah isn't up there?"

"Then *you* ask him."

In January of 1976 I climbed to a Cades Cove fire tower in the Smoky Mountains of Tennessee. This climb is a wonderful hike, a round trip of 10 miles. While hiking in the mountains I am so enthralled by the beauty of the trees and the wind—and especially the peace of it all—that I often burst out in praise to God. Many times while hiking I have broken out in song just thanking God for my ability to walk and that I can see and hear and appreciate His marvelous creation.

On this trip I thought of my earthly father, who died in 1955 at the age of 46. I wondered whether my father had surrendered his life to Jesus and was in heaven for eternity. Mother had told us that in the last year of Dad's life, while ill, he read the Bible all the way through. Surely, I thought, he knew his Savior personally. As I walked higher this day, the wind started to blow so hard that I truly had to plant my feet at times for fear of being blown over. The higher I climbed, the colder it became, and rain began to drip down through the trees. All I could do was praise and thank God for the beauty all around me. His power and His majesty overwhelmed me.

Surely by now you know that I believe the Bible is the Word of God and that events recorded therein happened just the way the Bible says they happened. For example, I also believe that:

- Jonah was thrown off a ship into the sea and swallowed by a great fish, and that the fish spat Jonah out of its mouth onto dry land.
- Peter was told by Jesus to catch a fish, take the coin from its mouth, and pay the temple tax with it.
- The walls of Jericho did fall down after the Israelites marched around the city seven times, blowing their horns just as God told them to do.
- When Jesus told Nicodemus he had to be born again to be saved, that's exactly what Jesus meant. Jesus explained to Nicodemus that a person had to be reborn spiritually, not physically.
- Jesus died on the cross for our sins and, because He did, we can have eternal life. All we have to do is look to the Son and believe in Him, and we will have eternal life. The Word of God says that He will raise us up on the last day. That's powerful Good News!

So there I was, high in the mountains praising God, when I suddenly felt a strong compassion for my dad. I believe that we may freely ask our earthly father—or heavenly Father in the name of Jesus—for anything. If we don't receive the thing we ask for, it's because it isn't the right thing for us at the time. I prayed this prayer to God in the name of Jesus, His Son.

> Dear Father in heaven, you know my earthly father, James Austin Hunt, who died 20 years ago. I don't know for sure that he knew your Son. Dear Father, I ask that you stop time and, if my dad was not saved, let time go back to where he can surrender his life to you. Give this man your Spirit so that he may have everlasting life. I believe whatever we ask in the name of Jesus is done, according to your holy will. I have faith that my dad is in heaven, and I believe God can stop time. Thank you, Father!

I guess we would have to say that is having faith like a child's. When we seek God daily to know His will, we draw closer to Him. As we draw closer to Him and we know that we are in His presence, our faith gets stronger. By reading the Word of God we bond with the Holy Spirit, who will guide us to be able to understand even more of the Word—and help our faith increase even more.

I once read that a very successful man wrote the following on a business card and kept the card in his wallet throughout his life. I copied it to do the same.

> God is who He said He is.
> God can do what He said He can do.
> I am who God says I am.
> I can do all things through Christ, who strengthens me.
> God's Word is alive and active in me.
> I'm believing God!

One day, while living in Gatlinburg, Tennessee, and hiking in the Smoky Mountains, I had an experience that I would like to share with you. As mentioned in Chapter 7, I had resigned from Pepe's Pizza (where I had worked for nine years) and moved to Gatlinburg, thinking I could write and support my family. I had planned to be there only one year, and already seven months were gone and I hadn't earned any money writing. In my spirit I believed I was to write a book called *It's Time to Change Your Values*. While hiking, I asked God to help me write this book. Now I know that when I need firewood I can pray for it, but I still will have to go out and cut it, or at least pick it up, and bring it home. This is what I heard in my Spirit, and it was so powerful that I still remember it after all these years. That was 1975; today is 2009. I had been praying in the Spirit and asking God for understanding, and this is what came out of my mouth: "Do your will through your will; I am in your will through your will."

> ***God loves us so much that when we surrender our will to His will, we become one with Him.***

This is what those words meant to me then and still mean today: God loves us so much that when we surrender our will to His will, we become one with Him. His will is our will, and our will is His will. We become as one! This means to me that I should do what I want to do because we are together as one. So if I want to write, I should go ahead and write. My will is His will, and His will is my will. This is truly being one with God in spirit

This is what faith is all about: *surrender, trust,* and *praise.* My brother Don wrote a book explaining *surrender, trust,* and *praise*, using (as I stated earlier) the name of the oil additive STP to help us remember the three important words. When you *surrender* your ideas, concerns, decision making, health, and family to God—and then *trust* that He will let things work out for your good, truly trusting God and stopping all worrying—you can then just *praise* and thank God for answering your prayers. Just thank God for being able to surrender whatever it is, as well as for your trust that He will bring peace and joy, however things turn out. Use *STP* in all facets of your life to attain true peace, confidence, and good health.

Many people live as though they're going to live forever ...

- "Next month I'll start eating right and exercising."
- "Next year I'll go to California."
- "Next year I'll start writing that book that I know is in me."

It's always in the future, not now but later. Plenty of time, we think.

Do we *have* plenty of time? I'm reminded of what we read in James 4:13–15:

> *Now listen, you who say, "Today or tomorrow we will go to this or that city, spend a year there, carry on business*

> *and make money." Why, you do not even know what will happen tomorrow. What is your life? You are a mist that appears for a little while and then vanishes. Instead, you ought to say, "If it is the Lord's will, we will live and do this or that."*

Should we pick up that phone or pen and tell that loved one we love him or her now, today? Should we now, right now, tell our Lord we love Him and ask for help for the day? Should we today ask God to take over our lives completely and surrender our wills over to Him? Should we now, today, do something about our extra weight and shortness of breath? Should we today pick up good books that will broaden our minds and help us be better people?

You have an obligation to yourself today to get right with God.

You have an obligation to yourself today to get right with God. Every day people are dying with sorrow because they put off important things they wanted to do someday, having let television, alcohol, computers, and foolishness waste their time. We all have the same 24 hours a day. Plan your day and work your plan. Put God first, and then set your goals.

Allow me to share a little story/poem I wrote in 1975.

> A young man's strength is fine to behold; surely all is his to unfold. He learns that to drink is Jolly, for how is he to know the Folly? The world says, "Drink up and be Jolly, for today may be your last day."
>
> If that young man really knew the Folly, would he waste his time and money? "Probably not," chimes in the Jolly.
>
> The question arises, Can a mind be pickled, like a cucumber is pickled? You bet. A mind can be pickled as surely as a cucumber is pickled. Where does the mind go when the mind is pickled? Ah yes, the mind goes nowhere when the mind is pickled, but time marches on, yes, on and on.
>
> One day, a young man is an old man: Time has passed him by, and why? That's the same question the old man asks himself: Why? It must be said that what he thought was being Jolly was just one big Folly. Now his life is not Jolly, because his life was spent in Folly.

If there is something to learn from this story, it is this: If you had the last cucumber in the world, would you pickle it or use it to grow more cucumbers? Since you have only one mind, will you pickle it or use it to further mankind?

The buck stops with you! You are responsible for your own life—and your eternal life.

Your answer is entirely up to you; the choice is neither my obligation nor that of your wife or husband, church, pastor, sisters, or brothers. No one can give an answer for you; it is up to you to make the choice. The buck stops with you! You are responsible for your own life—and your eternal life.

In prayer ask God for faith. Listen to men and women of faith as often as possible. Read books that strengthen your faith. As I mentioned earlier, Merlin Carothers' book *Prison to Praise* is one I strongly recommend.

Ask Jesus to take over your life, and surrender everything to His will. Just lay yourself at His feet and turn over your life to His will. When you do this you will know that Jesus is alive and the Bible is the Word of God. Then read all of John and Acts in the New Testament, and your faith will blossom.

The following was written by my wife, Cheryl, in May 1976.

Cheryl left us for her heavenly reward in June 2008.

God Gave Us Jesus

God gave us Jesus,
What wonderful news.
He is within us,
That is Good News.

There is no waiting,
He's right here and now.
Just accept Him, and then praise Him,
And He'll come in with a POW!

Knowing Him will change you;
No longer will you seek
For things in the past,
When your spirit was so weak.

When we give in to sin—
Being human we still do—
We look to Him more often
Than we used to.

Knowing at that moment
That I'm sorry is just enough,
For He already forgave us
That day they were so rough.

What is Faith? It's knowing
He'll answer every call.
Just knock, and the door will open
Whether the need is large or small.

Now how are we to do this?
Just ask it "in my name"
As Jesus Himself tells us
In the Bible, the book of fame.

Let us share in His life by loving
And giving Him all we can,
And we will see His shining face in Heaven
And complete His plan.

Having faith like a child's is not easy. God told Moses that he was to free all the Israelites from Egypt and lead them to the Promised Land. Moses tried his best to get out from under the orders he received from God, but in the end he acquiesced. Moses led the people of Israel out into the desert. Now what was he going to do with them? What would've happened had Moses tried to figure out what was needed to accomplish God's plan—and try to do it himself?

One of the biggest arithmetical miracles in the history of the world—past and present—was required to feed all those people. They had to be fed, and feeding 3½ million people required a lot of food. In Exodus 12:37 we learn that there were 600,000 Israelite men, "besides women and children." So, based on average family size in that era, an estimate of 3½ million is reached. The Bible also says the Children of Israel were given manna (a form of bread) from heaven and quail in great numbers. There is no mention of any other type of food.

According to calculations by a U.S. Army quartermaster general (whose job it is to supply soldiers on the battlefield), the Israelites needed 1,500 tons of food each day, enough to fill two freight trains. Listed below is what the Army says the Israelites would have needed had it been the supplier. Besides, you must remember the people were out in the desert and needed firewood to cook the food. This would have taken 4,000 tons of wood and a few more freight trains, each a mile long—just for one day! And they were 40 years in transit! Oh yes, they also needed water. Eleven million gallons of water would've been required each day, enough to fill a freight train of tanker cars 1,800 miles long, to provide just enough to drink and wash a few dishes.

Another thing: When the Israelites were leaving Egypt, they had to cross the Red Sea in one night. Now, if they had gone on a narrow path, double file, the line would have been 800 miles long, and 35 days and nights of travel would have been required to get through. So to get over in one night, as the Bible states, there had to be a corridor in the Red Sea three miles wide so they could walk 5,000 abreast. Finally, think about this: Every time the people camped at the end of the day, a campground more than half the size of Rhode Island was required, an area of 750 square miles.

Did Moses figure all this out before he left? I think not. You see, Moses believed in God. He had faith that God would take care of everything. Let us take courage; we have the same God!

– 16 –

Integrity

All through my life I have been taught the importance of honesty, also known as integrity. Integrity is one of the cornerstones of success in life. I recently read the story of Bernie Madoff, who managed billions of dollars for individuals and foundations. He was widely admired as an elder statesman on Wall Street. He held a coveted spot as chairman of a major stock exchange, NASDAQ. As has been revealed, however, Madoff was a charlatan of epic proportions who "made off" with $50 billion in stolen funds. He was a greedy manipulator so hungry for wealth that he didn't care whom he hurt in order to get what he wanted. He has confessed to choreographing a career-long scheme of theft on a mammoth scale. Now in his 70s, he has been found to have lived much of his life without integrity.

More than ever we are hearing of this very thing, an absence of integrity, which is bringing down people who were admired for years.

One day, when I was in seventh grade, my good friend Joe Nichols and I were riding home on our bikes after football practice, and we were thirsty. We noticed cases of Coke sitting next to a Coke machine at a gas station. The Coke machine was to the side of the building, out of sight of the office. We just went over and took a couple of Cokes, opened them, and left drinking them. When I arrived home dinner smelled so good, as Mother was an excellent cook and always had wonderful meals for all of us to eat together. At that time there were no fast-food franchises; we ate almost all our meals at home. The highlight of our day was sitting together eating and discussing sports, business, and happy things.

When I walked through the door, my father was waiting for me. He asked me to follow him to his office. We went in through the French doors, and he told me to shut the doors and sit. He asked me whether I had done anything that day that was not right in my eyes, that I wished I hadn't done. No, I responded,

I couldn't think of anything. He then told me that Mr. Bradley from the Shell station had phoned him to say that he saw my friend and me steal two Cokes. Dad said, "Son, I want you to go up to your room for the night; you'll miss dinner. I want you to think about what you did when you took something that didn't belong to you. Yes, it was only a nickel for each Coke, but it didn't belong to you. Never take something that doesn't belong to you. Tomorrow I expect you to go over to Mr. Bradley and tell him you're sorry you did this and pay him for the Cokes. Remember, anything you do reflects on the entire family."

I did go upstairs where I had time to do some hard thinking. Even as the aroma from supper wafted up the steps, I realized I had learned a lesson—one I would always remember.

There have been many instances in my business life with my brothers where we made decisions that cost us large sums of money, but they were decisions made on the side of integrity, which is an important part of my life. Always when I chose to go on the integrity side, no matter what the cost, I benefited as a person. Don't forget, we can't outgive God. Whatever we plant will come up as a harvest.

Maybe you've heard the story about the older man who frequented a small neighborhood grocery store in the 1930s. He was very likable, and the owner of the store admired and respected him as her regular customer. He always had something nice to say to make people feel good about themselves. Normally he paid with 20-dollar bills.

> *What does it profit a man if he gains the whole world yet loses his soul?*

One day the bank phoned the store owner to tell her she had deposited a counterfeit 20-dollar bill, which meant she would lose $20. Twenty dollars in the '30s had a lot of buying power. A few days later she received another call from the bank that she had deposited another fake twenty. The bank told her a federal agent would be over to visit her. The federal agent told her to try to keep records of who gave her 20-dollar bills the next week. She did, and sure enough she received some more counterfeit bills. The federal agent followed up on the people, and when he entered the apartment of the older man, he discovered the tools of his trade. In the man's home were the most beautiful paintings. The man was a gifted artist, but when the agent went up into his attic, he found where he was making his own 20-dollar bills. It had taken him hours to do each one by hand, and they were excellent.

Because of the man's lack of integrity, he chose to counterfeit, to steal. Yet, he ultimately stole from himself. You see, he had great talent and wasted his God-given talent for immediate reward.

Paraphrasing Mark 8:36, what does it profit a man if he gains the whole world yet loses his soul? It starts with the little things. U.S. author John Kabat-Zinn got it right when he said, "The little things? The little moments? *They aren't little.*"

Years ago when my children were young, I put the following in the downstairs bathroom. It is still on the wall in that bathroom. Author is unknown.

Strive for Integrity

Nothing, absolutely nothing, is more important to your future than personal integrity. Webster's defines it in one word—honesty. And you can only hide your lack of it for so long. Eventually, like a faulty foundation in a storm, the cracks will widen, the roof will fall in, and everything you've worked for will be lost. "Getting away with it" can be worse than getting caught, because it encourages you to believe that you can keep living at two levels. Listen: *"Like a partridge that hatches eggs it did not lay is the man who gains riches by unjust means ... In the end he will prove to be a fool"* (Jeremiah 17:11).

Don't think you can do whatever you want in small things and be OK as long as you have no major lapses. It's your first lie that makes you a liar. Whether you steal a dollar or a million dollars, you're still a thief. Nineteenth-century clergyman Phillips Brooks, who wrote the words to "O Little Town of Bethlehem," once said, "Character is made in the small moments of our lives." Integrity always puts character over personal gain, people over things, service over power, principle over convenience, and the long view over the immediate.

Every time you break a moral principle, it becomes harder, not easier, to act with integrity. Everything you've done in the past, including the things you've neglected to do, comes to a head when you're under pressure. That's why developing and maintaining integrity requires constant vigilance and discipline. John Weston said, "Live by the following rule: Don't do anything you wouldn't feel comfortable reading about in tomorrow's newspaper."

U.S. industrialist and philanthropist Andrew Carnegie said, "The older I get, the less I listen to what people say. I just watch what they do."

Here I have listed some things in everyday life that show integrity:

- Being honest about the stories of the happenings in your life.
- Paying back a loan, no matter the size.
- Fixing or replacing that piece of equipment you borrowed and broke.
- Not talking about others in a negative way.
- Giving others credit when they deserve it instead of taking credit yourself.
- Keeping your word even when it hurts.
- Paying people fairly for the work they do.

- Leaving your personal information on that car you gashed with your door.
- Choosing to stay true to your spouse throughout your marriage.
- Paying your taxes according to the law.
- Teaching your children integrity by example.
- Not cheating in your schoolwork.
- Doing what you say you will do in business.
- Not stealing towels or anything else from the hotels you use.
- Treating others with honesty and respect.

There are many other examples as well that could be given here, but the very best question to ask yourself in all situations is: *What would Jesus do?*

Hunt Brothers Pizza office/distribution center in Paris, Kentucky

Hunt Brothers Pizza participated in the 2012 National Association of Convenience Stores (NACS) Food Show in Las Vegas, Nevada. The HBP booth provided thousands of pizza samples and was one of the finest in the show.

Jim and Cheryl on their honeymoon in Florida in 1969

Yvette, Alexis, Erin, Adam, Zachary, Cheryl, Rachel, Jim, Frank, and Todd in 2002

Charlie, Don, Jim, and Lonnie

Lonnie, Elizabeth, Theresa, Jim, Mary, Charlie, and Don

Rachel Hunt (left) and Fehintola Oyeyemi (back right) pose with the children after church at the Peace and Love office in Lagos, Nigeria, in 2010.

Austin's on Highway 41 in Evansville, Indiana

Rev. Titus Oyeyemi with Jim in Lexington, Kentucky, in 2003

Jim (green cap at right) was privileged to participate with Rev. Oyeyemi (seated with red shirt) at the groundbreaking of the TimeOn Kairos Peace Institute in Lagos, Nigeria, in 2010.

– 17 –

ATTITUDE

2010

With the right attitude anything that happens can turn out well. Our attitudes when we wake up in the morning have a whole lot to do with the outcome of the day. William James said it well: "The greatest discovery of my generation is that a human can alter his life by altering his attitude."

All human beings, no matter their station in life, have challenges and difficult circumstances to deal with. These tough times and setbacks simply "come with the territory" of life. What I've come to realize is that it's not so much what happens to us, it's how we respond to it.

It so happens I had an attitude test going on once in a hotel. It was the off season in Sorrento, Italy, and I was in one of the finest small hotels in the world. With 56 rooms the hotel put a family right next to me with a baby that wouldn't stop crying. Evidently the parents believed, like Cheryl and I did, that you don't pick up the baby every time the infant cries. So, after adjusting my attitude, and remembering our years traveling and staying in hotels, and the people who might have wished that *our* family was not right next door to them, I relaxed and had peace. Also, I thought about the young family with their baby and the wonderful years Cheryl and I had raising our children. I said a prayer for the family. A good attitude can make all the difference.

A good attitude can make all the difference.

I remember one instance when my attitude made the difference for the success of the whole day. It was winter and cold. I had loaded my commercial van the night before in order to leave Paris, Kentucky, at 6 a.m. My truck was full of pizza product. I even had to put boxes on the passenger's seat and could barely see the mirror on that side. On that day I was in the process of developing a wholesale pizza route from

Paris to Pound, Virginia. Normally, after servicing my existing accounts and opening new accounts, I would reach my motel in Pound around 1 a.m., but an hour out of Paris that morning, my van's driveshaft fell out.

Now at that point I could have "lost it," but, by the grace of God, I didn't. There were no cell phones in those days, so I had to get to a phone. I called the company that serviced my vehicles in Paris, and a tow truck was sent to pick me up and drag me back to Paris, an hour away. The company didn't have the replacement driveshaft and said it would be the next day before the van could be fixed. I rented a truck and unloaded the van into the rented truck. Finally, around noon, I was ready to start again. I had joy and peace because my attitude was right. I knew I was running late and would be out longer the next day, but all I could do was service one account at a time, and all would be well.

How many times have we been driving down the road on an interstate highway and noticed we were short on fuel? Again, we can panic, or we can turn the problem over to God. I try to ask myself, *What is the worst thing that can happen in this situation?* In the case of running out of fuel, the worst that can happen is running out and having to walk or hitch a ride to get more. Because of my attitude, I seldom get upset, and my day isn't ruined.

I discovered early in my marriage to Cheryl that she wasn't always ready to leave our home at the time we had both agreed to leave. Maybe some of you men who are married understand what I'm talking about. For many years this was a problem for me. You see, my attitude toward this wasn't good. But later on there were times when my attitude improved. I relaxed and didn't give Cheryl my thoughts about us leaving late. Something I noticed over the years—and while traveling Europe with Cheryl—was that her sense of timing was lower key than mine, yet we accomplished just as much. When I realized this, I changed my attitude, and it was more pleasant for everyone to be around me.

How do you respond when a restaurant serves you something that isn't right or its service isn't up to your expectations? It may not even be the waitress's fault but instead the chef's. So many people blow it by getting angry at the waitress. The right attitude will allow you to handle disagreement in a way that the waitress will appreciate you and will be happy to make things right for you. By thinking of how hard restaurant people work and the long hours they put in for such little pay, the right attitude should kick in. Many are single mothers trying to support their children on a small income. When I think of these things, I want to give them extra-large tips and treat them with the respect they deserve. My understanding of their situation affects my attitude toward them.

> This morning the sky here in Sorrento is beautiful.
> Mount Vesuvius is clearly seen, and it has snow on top.
> It's beautiful. My attitude is excellent!

While in the hospital for a three-day stay some years ago, I had a roommate who was an African American pastor. The first morning in the room with him, I woke up to him singing the following prayer. What a tremendous way to start the day. This kind of prayer changes attitudes and helps the day ahead be a joyful one. I now attempt to pray it daily.

> Dear God, as I begin this day
> Let me turn my thoughts to you

And ask your help in guiding me
In everything I say and do.

Give me the patience that I need
To keep my peace of mind,
And with life's cares I hope, dear God,
Some happiness to find.

Let me live but for today
Not worrying what's ahead,
For I have trust that you will see
I get my daily bread.

Give me courage to face life's trials
And not from trouble run;
Let me keep this thought in mind:
Thy will, not mine, be done.

And if some wish I do not get,
Though I have prayed to thee,
Help me to believe and understand
You know what's best for me.

I've failed you many times, I know,
But when tonight I rest,
I hope that I can kneel and say,
"Dear God, I've tried my best."

In Jesus' name, amen.

In January 2011, I was on the island of Bonaire, which, on October 10, 2010, became a public entity within the Kingdom of the Netherlands and was no longer part of the Netherlands Antilles. The kingdom also changed to the U.S. dollar as its currency. I stayed in the same condominium the queen of the Netherlands stays in when she visits. Bonaire is 50 miles north of Venezuela, 86 miles east of Aruba. It is considered a diver's paradise because of its pristine waters, stunning coral reefs that encircle the island just feet from shore, and other spectacular marine life. The island of Bonaire is only 24 miles long and anywhere from 50 feet to seven miles wide. It is populated by Dutch, French, South American, and African people.

After leaving Bonaire I spent two weeks in Curaçao, a small Dutch island just 30 miles from Bonaire. Another attitude adjustment was necessary. The Avila Hotel is beautiful, with its wonderful beach and all the amenities. I arrived at the hotel around 3 p.m., and the hotel clerk said it would be about an hour before my room was ready. I hadn't eaten that day, so I took that time to have lunch and do some reading. After an hour or so I returned to the check-in desk and was given a key to a room. When I entered the room the hotel gave me, what I found was a man working on his computer. The room was very nice, with a good view of the ocean, but it was apparent I wasn't supposed to be in that room.

I returned to the hotel desk and explained there was a man in the room doing work on his computer. The staff admitted the mistake and gave me a key to another room. On entering the room I noticed it was in the back of the complex, and just below me was the kitchen. Four men were washing pans and making a lot of noise talking and laughing. Also, upon walking out onto the balcony I found there was no view of the water or sound of the ocean. I returned to the desk and explained that this wouldn't work for me and I didn't like the room I was assigned, as I would be in Curaçao two weeks and I expected to be close to the ocean. My attitude was very good, and the staff's was also. I was assured a satisfactory room would be found for me. I went over to the lobby and sat down and waited for more than an hour, reading while I was waiting. Finally the manager came over and sat down next to me and thanked me for my patience. He said I had received an upgrade to a room that I would surely appreciate. It was excellent, and I had a wonderful stay.

Because my attitude was right I had no heart palpitations, no anxiety, no hot flashes. I was just calm, and everything worked out.

What follows is another example of attitude adjustment. In February 2011, I was on the small island of Tortola in the British Virgin Islands. The villa I was staying in wasn't what I expected, based on its Internet site and the explanation my otherwise excellent travel agent had given me.

> *Because my attitude was right I had no heart palpitations, no anxiety, no hot flashes. I was just calm, and everything worked out.*

The beach was very small and blocked off on each end, which didn't allow a long walk. The restaurant wasn't on the water but inside the complex; it was more like a delicatessen. My room did have a wonderful balcony right on the ocean looking at the islands St. Martin and St. John (the latter is a U.S. territory). The breezes were wonderful, and the room had plenty of glass looking out of the kitchen and living room area. My main problem with the room was the bedroom. It was situated in the back of the villa. No windows! Also, when in the bedroom I couldn't hear the surf right under the balcony, which was located in the front. There were light bulbs that needed to be replaced in the kitchen area and the bathroom area, and the lamps by the sofa were so dim I couldn't read by them. Further, the ceiling fan was so high I couldn't reach the switch, and I couldn't find a wall switch for remote control. So, I thought about this the first night and decided to talk to the manager in the morning. I figured if I didn't like what was offered, I would find a different hotel.

After I explained my thoughts to Pamela, the manager, who listened to all my complaints with a concerned smile, she explained there were no rooms with a bedroom on the ocean. I then said that in that case I would check out of the villa. She told me I would lose the money I had paid in advance. I said

I would phone the credit card company and explain that the resort was falsely advertised.

Pamela then said she was a problem solver and felt we could resolve this. She asked me whether I would be willing to look at a couple of other rooms. All our conversation, by the way, was calm. Neither she nor I showed any ill will. We looked at another room, which was an upgrade, but the bedroom was in the back; therefore the offering didn't help at first. I told Pamela if the sofa was a sofa bed, the room would work for me. She said the sofas were not sofa beds, but she said we could move the *bed* to the front—to the living room—and then I would have all the balcony windows, glass doors, and ocean to wake up to. I said that would work for me. She agreed to replace all the light bulbs and showed me where the ceiling fan wall switch was, and I was happy. The long walk on the beach wasn't available, but the beach and pier were beautiful. The restaurant ended up working out OK, since I ate most meals elsewhere anyway. Because Pamela's attitude was good and mine was on overdrive, we hugged and were happy campers.

As a teacher of employees and a trainer of sales personnel, I've discovered that training a person who has an upbeat attitude motivates me to be the best I can be. On the other hand, I've found that being with a person who has a "downer" attitude can pull me down if I'm not careful. In the latter case, it's a very short time before I stop everything and get eye to eye with the chap. I explain to him what I see and feel—and try to get to the bottom of why he is unresponsive and acting so negatively. I want to help the person understand that if he is going to work with us, there must be a significant change immediately or we will need to part company.

You see, it's all about self-discipline. You must discipline yourself to have enthusiasm. As Norman Vincent Peale said in his book *Enthusiasm Makes the Difference,* you must "act enthusiastic to become enthusiastic." You can wake up feeling good or bad based on your attitude. You determine the outcome of your day because you have control of your life by way of a positive attitude. A positive person wakes up saying, "Today *is* a great day" or "Thank you, Jesus, that I woke up today. Help me be all you want me to be today." Today is another opportunity for you to be the best you can be. The well-known cliché is actually true: Today is the first day of the rest of your life.

You can control your mood for the day—indeed, for your life—by having a positive attitude. If you look in the mirror and smile, you will see yourself smiling back. It sure beats a frown. If you smile at the people you meet throughout the day, you may be pleasantly surprised by the number of returned smiles you receive.

> *A kind word to people you meet throughout the day will be a blessing to them and to you.*

Fathers and mothers: A simple, sincere, kind word to your spouse and children is so valuable. In your relationships the discipline to develop your listening skills is most important. You need to listen to better understand so that when you speak you will be understood. Your attitude when listening to your spouse is vital for a good marriage. A kind word to people you meet throughout the day will be a blessing to them and to you. As I've said before, you can't outgive God, and when you give love to others you will reap a harvest in return.

Even your food digests better when your mood is good. Your whole body responds to your mood. Studies have shown that individuals with a serious illness or undergoing surgery have a better chance of recovery when their attitude is positive.

It takes discipline to keep your mood or attitude "up," but the benefits are astronomical. It's the difference between night and day, sour and sweet, hell and heaven. Yes, between hell and heaven, because keeping your attitude positive does make a tremendous difference in your marriage and your entire life.

Even your food digests better when your mood is good. Your whole body responds to your mood.

You can break bad habits, but you must want

to do so. Don't let any one thing become master of your life. From the time I was 15 years of age until I was 55, I smoked cigars and pipes. At 55 I had a heart attack and bypass surgery. I was told not to smoke or be around smoke. This was enough for me to stop smoking. There was a period of time I had to go through when I considered smoking but chose not to. For years now I have had no desire to smoke, nor do I want to be around anyone who is smoking.

Abuse of wine, beer, and the hard stuff also can be a serious problem in our lives. It may not seem to be a problem when we're younger, but it can become a detriment to our true success in life. Alcohol can ruin our family lives, our business futures, and our personal relationships. At this time of my life I would say to my children and grandchildren that drinking is best left out of your lives. I am concerned about the alcohol-related brain damage that we read about, as well as the waste of time, money, and mental capacity associated with drinking. If we find that drinking has taken away our self-control, then it's time to stop. Anything that masters us is not good for us. When I made the decision to stop smoking, I stood by my decision. Now it isn't a concern to me at all, and my life is cleaner and healthier.

> *Like a city whose walls are broken down is a man who lacks self-control.*
>
> —Proverbs 25:28

I would like to share with you how the right attitude helped me and two of my adult children overcome a life-or-death situation. In March 2012 my daughter Rachel and my son Todd were with me in Amalfi, Italy. We were in a restaurant enjoying a wonderful meal when the waitress suggested we might enjoy a hike on the Path of the Gods (Sentiero Degli Dei). She made it sound like a nice trail that families walked all the time. Since we were walking a couple of hours each day, this hike was something we wanted to do.

The next day we took a bus up to Agerola, which is high above Amalfi. This was where the 3½-hour hike started. The Path of the Gods is from Agerola to Positano on the Amalfi coast. We started about 2 p.m. and eventually arrived at a dangerous-looking place. To our right a trail continued steeply up a mountain. To our left, down a narrow path, was a village and the ocean, both of which looked like they were miles down. We then saw a sign with a painted-on arrow pointing straight ahead and up a small rise. We made the decision to go that way, thinking we would eventually be going down instead of up and—we hoped—to the left toward the ocean.

It turned out we had no business on the trail we had chosen. We had made a bad mistake. Our innocent little hike had become mountain climbing! We were on segments of a trail that were 2 feet wide above cliffs dropping straight down. We came to places where we had to walk sideways and put our hands on the side of the mountain. At times we actually sat down to move on the trail. We seriously thought that one of us might fall off. It started to get dark, and we realized we might have to spend the night on the mountain. We prayed and just kept going. Our attitude was that we had no choice, no one could help us, we had to go forward. Rachel and Todd were so brave, and no one complained.

Just as it was getting dark we saw olive trees and a shack. No one was around, but this gave us some hope. A few hundred yards past there, we came to a church. We decided to go a little bit farther, and if it got too dark, we could spend the night in the church. Just past the church we saw steps going down. Stone steps 4 feet wide. *How did the Italians do this, and who would walk this far up a mountain to a church?* I asked myself. We walked down the steps in the dark. It must have been a mile and a half to the village of Praiano. From there we caught a bus down to Amalfi on the ocean. We walked more than five hours on that trail. I believe that as we faced death our attitudes—and prayers—helped keep us safe.

– 18 –

Forgive Yourself

2010

At this time in my life I teach classes on a volunteer basis at an organization called Lighthouse Ministries in Lexington, Kentucky. Mrs. Valerie Henderson and her husband, who is now deceased, started this wonderful facility. Tay, as Valerie is known by all who love her, is the strong leader of this growing ministry. It is completely dedicated to helping men with addictions put their lives back together. Most of the men have served time in prison or experienced homelessness. Their present and future lives are in jeopardy. Some have a wife and children. Some initially became addicted after taking pain medicine, then moved into deeper addictions. A number of the men were in responsible positions before their habits took control. Some lost their families because of addiction.

As volunteers and staff, our purpose is to pray with them through a program of 6–12 months where they live at the Lighthouse and attend three to four classes a day on life and Scripture. The Lighthouse residents also serve 80–100 homeless people hot lunches daily. It is a blessing for them to be able to serve people who have sunk to the level of homelessness, knowing they themselves were headed there or had already been there.

One of the most important teachings at the Lighthouse is that the men must forgive themselves, as well as forget and forgive their past mistakes. It's difficult for most of them to forgive themselves and, as you listen to their stories, you can understand why it's hard for them to do so. Some have been in and out of jail many times. Almost all have been in jail at least once. When drugs get the best of a person, all he can think about is doing whatever it takes to get more. This means in many instances stealing the very money needed for his family's food and shelter and schooling. Stealing and lying become a compulsion that the drug addict is helpless to control. He hurts his parents, his brothers and sisters, his children. Family relationships in many cases are damaged or even destroyed.

When the addicted person can honestly understand the Good News that Jesus died for all his sins and that He doesn't see them anymore, as though they never existed, the person is brought new hope. There's a cleansing that only Jesus can bring to that person. When this happens, the individual can stand tall again and live with himself and know he can go forward and ask forgiveness of those he has hurt. He knows he can once again have a new life, a good life, a family, and a future.

Those of us who haven't had such addictions are fortunate indeed, but we're all sinners. Each of us has something that is a problem (maybe multiple problems) in our life.

Those of us who haven't had such addictions are fortunate indeed, but we're all sinners. Each of us has something that is a problem (maybe multiple problems) in our life. Something that gets in the way of us having joy each and every day. It may be the tongue, the use of that muscle that is so hard to control. (For more on the tongue, see the next chapter.) The wonderful thing we must remember is that Jesus continues to love us despite knowing that we will still sin. If our deepest desire is to follow Jesus and pray to do His will always, then we are on the right track. Our sins are forgiven, even our future sins, so long as we're always earnestly seeking to stay in God's will. God knows our hearts.

Whatever it is that steals your daily joy is, as we used to say in the '60s, a "bummer." But praise and thank Jesus for the problem (and what you can learn from it), and get on with your life. If you've lied to someone, ask the person to forgive you, ask God to forgive you, and move on with your life. If you've lost your temper, and it wasn't for a good reason, ask forgiveness and go on. If your problem is a moral one, ask God for forgiveness, and go on with your life. Don't let the devil take away your joy. He is a thief and a liar who wants to destroy your joy. In the name of Jesus, keep him behind you and make life-giving choices that give you a fresh start.

your joy. In the name of Jesus, keep him behind you and make life-giving choices that give you a fresh start.

– 19 –

The Power of the Tongue

2011

Oh, the things we can say if we don't control our tongue. Once they're said, they can't be taken back. They're in the air for all time. They go out like radio waves and never stop. People who hear them may well remember them the rest of their lives. For many of us, abuse of the tongue is a serious bad habit or addiction that hurts those we love—and in many cases destroys family relationships and, yes, marriages. We may not go to prison, but we may feel like we're in prison when we lose the ones we love because we can't control our tongue. If you don't believe me, read James 3:1–12!

> *Not many of you should presume to be teachers, my brothers, because you know that we who teach will be judged more strictly. We all stumble in many ways. If*

anyone is never at fault in what he says, he is a perfect man, able to keep his whole body in check.

When we put bits into the mouths of horses to make them obey us, we can turn the whole animal. Or take ships as an example. Although they are so large and are driven by strong winds, they are steered by a very small rudder wherever the pilot wants to go. Likewise the tongue is a small part of the body, but it makes great boasts. Consider what a great forest is set on fire by a small spark. The tongue also is a fire, a world of evil among the parts of the body. It corrupts the whole person, sets the whole course of his life on fire, and is itself set on fire by hell.

All kinds of animals, birds, reptiles and creatures of the sea are being tamed and have been tamed by man, but no man can tame the tongue. It is a restless evil, full of deadly poison.

With the tongue we praise our Lord and Father, and with it we curse men, who have been made in God's likeness. Out of the same mouth come praise and cursing. My brothers, this should not be. Can both fresh water and salt water flow from the same spring? My brothers, can a fig tree bear olives, or a grapevine bear figs? Neither can a salt spring produce fresh water.

How many times do we wish we could take back the words we speak? If only we had walked out of the room instead of shooting off our mouth. The next morning the disagreement is seen as nothing more than a petty argument that should never have happened. How sorry we are for the words that don't have to be said!

How do you discipline yourself to not speak words you will be sorry about later? A suggestion would be to listen closely to what the other person is saying—everything that is being said—*before* you speak. Remember, there is never a good reason or justification for losing your self-control. Even Jesus showed anger, but He didn't lose self-control. He had a purpose in His anger (sometimes termed righteous indignation).

Always take the time to think before you speak. Love your neighbor as yourself. Speak words of encouragement to others. Keep joy in your heart. When Cheryl and I would have a disagreement, we would often end up making a joke out of it and laugh together, and our discord would melt away before it became a real argument.

We can't take our words back and, as I've said, they just keep going like radio waves, on and on through space. They can hurt worse than a slap in the face. Whoever said, "Sticks and stones will break my bones, but words will never hurt me" didn't

> *The quiet words of the wise are listened to more readily ...*

know what he was talking about. The Bible says we are responsible for every word that comes out of our mouth. The tongue is the most difficult part of your body to control. For example, useless joking, using another person as the buffoon or butt of a joke, is of no value—and can do lasting damage to a relationship. Discipline yourself to use words wisely. Pray for wisdom in this matter, as it's so important for your personal and business life. The quiet words of the wise are listened to more readily than the loud words of a fool (see Ecclesiastes 5:1–7). You don't want to be "hung by the tongue"! Francis Martin wrote a book called just that: *Hung by the Tongue*. I strongly recommend it to help you better understand the power—for both good and evil—of the tongue.

The Good News, as stated in the previous chapter, is that we can change. We can ask forgiveness of those we've hurt and then commit ourselves to controlling our tongue.

– 20 –

Determination

PERHAPS YOU WANT A CAREER in selling—or you want to be a doctor, nurse, dentist, chiropractor, astronaut, homemaker, actor, artist, singer, musician, hotel and restaurant manager, real estate professional, teacher, athlete, parent, outstanding grandparent, or maybe a lifeguard. Perhaps you're ready to settle down and you want a partner for life. Whatever you want is possible if you believe it is so and are determined to make it happen.

Determination means having a firm or fixed purpose. You can't get there if you don't know where you're going. You aren't even in the game if you don't have a definite goal to shoot for. So first I urge you to pray for direction. As I indicated earlier, God's will is your will so long as you are willing to be in His will. This means that while you may not be doing everything right according to the Bible, you have surrendered your life to God through Jesus, in your heart and mind, and your will is to do God's will. Your sins have been forgiven—past, present, and future. So if you have a strong desire to work as a doctor, or you want to be a lifeguard, then you must *surrender* this desire to God, *trust* that He will let it come to pass if it is in His will, and *praise* God daily as you work toward your goal.

If you want to catch a fish because it's the only way you can feed your family, you will be determined to stay there and fish until you catch your meal. That is true determination.

Procrastination can melt down your determination, and it's one of the biggest deterrents to your personal success.

Procrastination can melt down your determination, and it's one of the biggest deterrents to your personal success. Procrastination means postponing something that you know you need to do. You have a speech to give in a week, and you put off preparing for it until the night before. You have a goal to give so many presentations of your product in a given week, but you put off making those calls until the end of the week.

This is where the 80/20 rule comes into focus. Twenty percent of a sales team are determined to hit or pass their goals. They make up their minds the day they set their goals, immediately create their plans, and through determination stick to those plans.

The other 80% of the sales team are those who don't ever make up their minds to hit their goals, and of course don't hit their goals; those who determine to hit their goals but don't make plans, and thus don't hit their goals; and those who do determine to hit their goals and do make plans, but they procrastinate, putting off till later doing what needs to be done, and thus don't hit their goals.

I have found that putting off what we know has to be accomplished, whether it is giving a certain number of presentations or preparing for a speech, causes us to be in a state of worry about that thing we are not doing. Every day it hangs over our heads because we know we have to do it.

So, for this reason the very best way to handle things we need to do is to do them. Doing them before they are due is exhilarating and mind-clearing, and it is the way of the winner, the 20 percenter. Working on them ahead of time gives you time to go back over them and make them the best you can. By working on those things and getting them out of the way, you end up on top, in the position of the achiever, instead of in the middle or on the bottom.

I'm reminded of the poor guy who was going to join a procrastinators club—but he never got around to it. May you find the determination not to be like that guy!

– 21 –

Empathy

The need to have empathy for—and with—others can't be overemphasized. *The New Oxford American Dictionary* describes empathy as the ability to understand and share the feelings of another.

Having empathy has been important throughout my life in sales and management—and as a husband and father. I believe that I can sincerely feel the pain of another person's tragedy. I can't count the number of times people have shared with me stories about cancer or death or other tragedies that have happened in their lives. Because of my empathy and the fact that I have listened to people with sincere interest—and many times have prayed with them—I've developed lifelong friendships. I wasn't much of a hugger early in my life, but after finding Jesus I found myself hugging lots of times in appreciation and love for individuals. In our company, hugging is simply a way of life. One year, at our Christmas-weekend celebration, with more than 600 of our company's team members present, I suggested that all members of my company make it a point to hug everyone they met all weekend. It truly made a difference in the love shown that weekend.

People in general don't show love, and it's needed more than ever today. It's sad to say this, but many men and women don't take the time to kiss and hug their spouse as they leave home each day. They usually don't take the time to tell their children and spouse they love them. In our family whenever we left home we would hug and kiss. Before going to bed we prayed together and hugged and kissed. Even today all my children hug me and kiss me when they come into the house for a visit or leave the house after a visit. We don't know whether we'll wake up the next day after going to bed or come home after an outing, so why not show that love each time we part company?

– 22 –

How Do We Know Our Purpose in Life?

Dear Yvette, Erin, Frank, Todd, Rachel, Adam, Alexis, and Zachary,

Your father is a follower of Jesus, as well as a salesman, businessman, teacher, disciplinarian, and lover of your mother. Your mother is a follower of Jesus, as well as a saleswoman, teacher, professional homemaker, special friend, nurse, cook, musician, imaginative storyteller, and lover of your father.

Many parents think their children should follow in the same paths of life as theirs, but your mother and I did our best not to push any particular path onto you. Some children will become parents, businesspeople, homemakers, artists, social workers, writers, or dietitians. All will become teachers because teaching happens on a daily basis in any of the above fields.

We also are salespeople. We're all selling ourselves daily in every area of our lives. I had to sell myself to Cheryl to date her and to ask her hand in marriage. Cheryl in turn sold herself to me while I was dating her. While in school we're selling ourselves to our fellow students and teachers. Everywhere we go we're selling ourselves.

How do we do this selling? By having a ready smile for everyone we meet. By going out of our way to be nice to people, even the strangers we come in contact with daily. We're selling ourselves by being on time for appointments or calling ahead if we'll be late. We're selling ourselves when others see our decisions are based on integrity. We're selling ourselves when we treat others fairly. We're selling ourselves when we control anger and show self-discipline. When we speak well of others rather than gossip about them. When we honor our financial debts by paying them on time. When we return something that we borrowed at the agreed-upon time and in the same or better condition. We're selling ourselves when we give to others who have needs without asking anything in return, even the dollars given.

> *Success is doing whatever gives you peace of mind on earth and leads you toward life eternal with God.*

The importance of these actions is what Cheryl and I as parents wanted to teach our children. How does this help us know what our purpose in life is?

The greatest blessing in life is to know what God wants us to do with the time we have on this earth. We must ask God for guidance as to our purpose in life. In the world, in the eyes of many, it seems wealth and material things make us successful, give us our purpose. In truth, success is a happy home, a loving spouse, and loving children. That can happen in the poorest home in Africa or the richest home in America.

A true definition of success is doing whatever gives you peace of mind on earth and leads you toward life eternal with God. How do we achieve success?

- Pray—trusting that God hears and answers prayer.

- Think—acting on your brainstorms.
- Share—quietly giving to others in response to what God has given to you.
- Be—becoming the man or woman you aspire to be in your own heart.

True happiness comes through giving and helping others. When you take your eyes off your own needs and wants and daily seek to be a blessing to others, you're on the way to happiness and peace. Ultimately, God has ingrained upon you the need to invest in eternal things. If you settle for investment in anything else, you won't find happiness.

Your purpose is to work in an area that you enjoy. Your work shouldn't seem like work to you; instead it's more like a hobby because you enjoy the work so

Your purpose is to work in an area that you enjoy. Your work shouldn't seem like work to you; instead it's more like a hobby because you enjoy the work so much.

much. And you should work where you're a blessing to others. Don't let money be your main reason for working in a particular field. First pray and decide exactly what you *want* to do daily, then do that as well as you can. If it's to write or work in some other artistic field, then discipline yourself to spend so many hours daily perfecting your talents and striving to be the very best writer or artist you're capable of becoming. Whatever field you choose, it's essential that you read up on and study your area of work in order to be the very best you can be. Be dedicated to your personal growth! Reading the Bible daily, as well as reading about the lives of others who have been successful, has always been a blessing to me and also has contributed to my personal growth and development of my talents.

Each of us is unique. God made each of us different, down to the hair on our head, our DNA, and our fingerprints. Our eyes and our voices can even be used to identify us. There are so many different parts of our bodies that can be used to identify us because each person is a miracle of God, unique.

God's plans for our lives also make us unique. He gave us the Holy Spirit to guide us daily. All we have to do is ask for His direction. *Surrender,* and ask the question; *trust* you will get an answer; and then *praise* God, thanking Him for the gift of the Holy Spirit. Each day and all through the day, thank the Holy Spirit for the answer you need. Your answer may come through a job offer or a friend who suggests an area of work. Be open to different ways your answer may come to you. When it comes, be sure to ask the Holy Spirit for assurance that it is His answer. We feel most satisfied and have true joy when we're doing what God wants us to do. Whatever you do in life, don't stand in the way of what God wants you to do. Remember, God can't use us until we're willing to let Him work through us.

Remember this all your life: If you want a harvest, you must plant seeds. This means that you must go out of your way to plant seeds. Plant seeds toward the need you have. Your harvest will be the result of the seeds you plant. The harvest from planting seeds of helping others, monetarily or physically, will satisfy your need, whatever it is—whether it's to find your purpose in life, to receive help in making a business decision, or to find the person God wants you to marry. Plant the seeds of your time, money, and service, then tell your Father in heaven exactly what kind of harvest you expect from that planting. The writer of Hebrews urges us to boldly approach the throne of grace, through our great High Priest, Jesus Himself:

> *Let us then approach the throne of grace with confidence, so that we may receive mercy and find grace to help us in our need.*
>
> —Hebrews 4:16

Many times I have planted seeds of money with people who had financial needs, telling God that I was planting those seeds toward the growth of the business or toward my unmarried children finding the perfect mates for life. Planting seeds toward your need is important for a happy, peaceful, fruitful life.

Money is necessary, and it can make your life more peaceful and fruitful. But in the end, when all is said and done, you want to be happy in the work you do. Money won't do it. I believe if you're doing what you truly enjoy and you don't recognize it as work because you enjoy it so much, then the money will follow.

> *Many are the plans in a man's heart, but it is the Lord's purpose that prevails.*
>
> —Proverbs 19:21

God has given you the desire and power to do His good purpose. God has determined your beginning and your end and the exact place for you in life. Live your life knowing that the best place to be is in the center of God's will. In this way you can be satisfied and have true joy.

> *Each one should use whatever gift he has received to serve others, faithfully administering God's grace in its various forms. If anyone speaks, he should do it as one speaking the very words of God. If anyone serves, he should do it with the strength God provides, so that in all things God may be praised through Jesus Christ. To him be the glory and the power for ever and ever. Amen.*
>
> —1 Peter 4:10–11

You are happiest when you are doing what God has designed you to do. His will should be your will; therefore, do the thing you want to do. So long as it is in line with loving God and loving your neighbor, you will be in His will.

Here is a beautiful prayer from Scripture (paraphrased by Bruce Wilkinson in his book *The Prayer of Jabez*) to help us in seeking God's will for our careers in life:

And Jabez called on the God of Israel, saying, "Oh that you would bless me indeed, and enlarge my territory for your glory, that your hand would be with me, and that you would keep me from evil, that I may not cause pain ..."

—1 Chronicles 4:10
(paraphrase by Bruce Wilkinson)

– 23 –

How to Help a Company Hire You

We are way ahead of the game if we know what we like to do and where we want to work. We generally like to do the things that we do well. The hard part is finding the company that will hire you to do what you like doing.

Through the years I have hired and trained many men and women. Many times it was the persistence of an individual—a strong desire to work with us, continued inquiries by phone about the position, and an enthusiastic interest in the company—that resulted in him or her being hired. When people show this kind of drive, it's very hard for a company to ignore them.

Case in point. Recently, while I was eating at a restaurant on the island of Bonaire, my waitress was especially attentive to how she served me and was particularly appreciative of my presence there. I assumed that she was an owner or a member of the ownership family. I asked her whether she was an owner, and she said no, she was an employee. She then took the time to tell me how much she enjoyed working there. She said the manager was a good person and knew his job. She went on to say that the chef was one of the best on the island and that the restaurant had been passed down through three generations. She told me about the great-grandfather and the grandfather and the present owner of the business. It was remarkable that she knew so much about where she worked. This young lady had made a decision to be enthusiastic and show pride in her company. In my opinion she will either go on to a more advanced position there or be hired for someone else's business. Incidentally, she appreciated the large tip I was happy to give her.

> *My advice is to study companies that employ people doing the kind of work you want to do.*

My advice is to study companies that employ people doing the kind of work you want to do. As the waitress in Bonaire did, learn all about them—their histories, the names of their officers, their yearly sales volumes, how many employees they have, and whether they have integrity. Study 5–10 companies this way to give yourself increased success at being hired. Decide which is the No. 1 company you would like to work with, then number the others in order of preference.

The next step is to send a well-written letter to the HR (human resources) person at the No. 1 company. Address the HR person by name. The letter should state clearly that you have studied the company and want to work with it—not *for* it but *with* it. If you have studied the company properly, you will know the CEO's name and history. Mention that you have studied the CEO's history and believe the CEO to be a person of fairness and integrity, and that this is one of your reasons for wanting to work with the company. State the type of position you desire, but note that you would be willing to start anywhere in the company, at whatever pay, in order to prove yourself. State that you will be the most enthusiastic, motivated, and dedicated person in the company. State also that you have a lifetime record of unmarred honesty, integrity, and hard work—that when you work with a company, you think like an owner and treat the customer like a king. Along with your letter send your résumé, a picture of yourself looking your best (men, this means suit and tie) and, if you're married, a picture of your spouse and any children.

Five days after mailing your letter, phone the HR person. Ask whether your letter was received. If he or she says it hasn't been read yet, state why you want to work with the company and that it's the one you most want to work with. Thank the HR person for taking the time to talk to you, and tell him or her you are most eager to hear back. If you aren't contacted the next day, phone the person again and ask whether you may come in and introduce yourself so you can show how sincerely you desire to work with the company. Every other day for a week phone the HR person for an interview until he or she interviews you or insists that you stop calling.

If the efforts directed at the first-choice company don't work in your favor and land you a position, then go to company No.

2 and on down the list until you're hired. Don't forget to use STP—*surrender, trust,* and *praise.*

– 24 –

How to Work for a Company

Do your work with pride as though you own the company. Take ownership of whatever you are paid to do. If you sweep and mop the floors and clean the bathrooms, do the best job you can. If you work for someone, don't talk negatively about him. If you have what in your mind is a very serious disagreement (philosophically or otherwise) with the management, then it's probably best to find work somewhere else.

All companies want happy, enthusiastic, responsible people working with them and with their customers. People who:

- Come to work with energy and vitality.
- Show they enjoy their work and appreciate and enjoy their colleagues.

- Are ready to help others when help is needed—and are willing to do whatever it takes to get a job done, including putting in extra time.
- Do a job right the first time, with minimal supervision.
- Are clean and wear appropriate clothes.
- Are complimentary to each other when at work.
- Speak well of management to those outside the company.

Seniority has little bearing on advancement in this day and age.

In order to increase your income as an employee of any company, you must be willing to take on more responsibility. Seniority has little bearing on advancement in this day and age. Study material that will educate you in the career you have chosen. Learn all you can about the responsibilities of your immediate supervisor. Prepare yourself to be able to take over your supervisor's position and that of his or her supervisor. Listen to motivational and educational recordings when you're driving. Attend teaching seminars and absorb the speakers' words and the manner in which they present their ideas. Learn from those speakers so you can be a better speaker in public and in business meetings. I strongly recommend that you attend a Zig Ziglar public speaking program or join Toastmasters to acquire the tools and confidence needed to be an outstanding presenter. Put this good stuff into your mind daily, and you will find it will help you all through life.

The decision to be a person of integrity is a no-brainer—and puts you on the path to financial stability. It's important that you have someone who holds you accountable to that decision. In my life, my brothers and sisters have held me accountable. I have listened to their advice, and it has held true. There have been times when it didn't make financial sense to do the right thing, but by doing the right thing I had peace of mind. Stand up and say so when you're wrong and accept the blame. In my life, I've preferred to give the credit to my team when we've done something outstanding. When a bad decision that affected the company has been made, I've taken the blame because I determined that the buck would stop with me.

As for loyalty, owners and management of companies treasure employees who have it, plus all the attributes I've discussed above. As for doing whatever it takes to get a job done, in my experience the person who does more than he or she is paid for throughout a career will eventually find reward at the end of the rainbow: a pot of gold.

– 25 –

Running My Business as Though I Were in a Wheelchair

BUILDING A PROFITABLE BUSINESS is not for the faint of heart. It takes dedication and persistence. In the early years of developing my business, I serviced my customers myself, which had me driving a minimum of 1,000 miles a week. While servicing those regular customers weekly, I opened new accounts. I did necessary paperwork each evening, monthly financial reports, and my own profit-and-loss statements; ordered product weekly; loaded product into the warehouse; and inventoried monthly. During that time Cheryl and I were bringing six of our eight children into the world. We enjoyed every minute of having a family and a business—both of which were growing!

But when I had the van accident near Sadieville, Kentucky (the time I jumped a ditch and became stuck on the side of a hill), I heard God tell me in my spirit to run my business as though I were in a wheelchair, and I did just what He told me to do.

The accident, and my response to God, happened around 1984. I soon hired a person to run my route and service my customers. I trained him well and made sure he understood my principles of business, which included treating others as one wanted to be treated (yes, Jesus' Golden Rule also applies to business). I then spent my time managing this employee and developing new business. I found I had the time to hire more men to run operations in the new areas I spread into.

After some time I was fortunate to hire Curtis Caudill from Whitesburg, Kentucky, a man of integrity and to this day a cherished friend and brother in Christ. In time Curtis was able to open and personally supervise 12 new areas. Also during this time Sally Wilder came aboard, took over office responsibilities, and managed the company as though she owned it. Sally hired office staff as we needed them and computerized us when the time came to do so. Sally was certainly a major reason why we were able to grow; she freed me up completely.

During the time Curtis was developing new areas, John Santos from Knoxville, Tennessee, was brought into the business. John also was very responsible and loyal and went on to develop another dozen areas and managed them completely. John was "a man on fire" and was another major reason we grew exponentially. During the company's growth I always tried to treat my employees as brothers and sisters. Our pay rate for team members was above the norm, and we treated them like family. We showed our appreciation at every opportunity.

Most of us can achieve more if someone believes in us. Those of you in a position of leadership: Give your people the chance to be everything they can be. Inspire them, motivate them, compliment them, and pray for them. Don't talk down to them or about them behind their backs. I learned long ago that if you're at the point where you're often talking negatively about a person, it's past time to go your separate ways.

From 1984 to the present year 2012, I have run my business as though I were in a wheelchair. As I've noted, when you're in a wheelchair you depend on others and appreciate them more. Communicating to people that you depend on them is a marvelous way to build them up. It gives people the chance to be more than they ever thought they could be. People want to achieve things, to go home proud of what they do each day. In early 2011 I was fortunate to be able to spend two weeks on the island of Bonaire, after which I flew to the island of Curaçao for two more weeks, then it was on to the island of Tortola in the British Virgin Islands for a final two weeks. I tell you this because I was confident I had good people running the business, who didn't need me around all the time. When I'm away I do, however, study the monthly financials, and we have monthly management meetings that keep the team members accountable to their commitments.

People want to achieve things, to go home proud of what they do each day.

Although I've spent many years figuratively operating the company from a wheelchair, I've tried to stay very alert to everything that goes on in each area of it. I've had a lot to say regarding growth and management. For many years I've planned and led sales meetings. I've held the positions of Sales Director, CEO, and COO. Most of the physical labor has been delegated to others. I also grew and ran my business as though I were a general. A military general must depend on his people. At this stage of my business life, I'm a mentor, the chairman of my company. We have very capable people in the positions of CEO, Sales Director, Comptroller, HR Director, Administrative Manager, and all of our office and warehouse personnel, along with our outstanding sales teams in the field.

Each of us brothers is owner of our own pizza business, but in 1990 we came together in Lexington and formed a new company. Each of us decided to continue to own and operate our own businesses, yet form a mother company called Hunt Brothers Pizza—with a team guiding all the companies through marketing, purchasing, training schools, research and development, information technology, and food shows.

The past 22 years we've been selling the same product and operating as one company. Four of my eight children are in the business, and each is doing a great job. Being a Hunt does not assure one of a position; there must be a need and a talent to fill that need. I'm very proud and appreciative of all the fine people working alongside us in Hunt Brothers Pizza.

What this style of management did was allow me to spend more time with Cheryl as we raised our children. It allowed me to be home with the family much more than most men.

No matter how much management we have, the most important person in the company is the one who sees the customers each week.

I realized early in my sales career that I didn't want an office at my distribution center. Since the beginning of my business, I have had my office at home. But having a home office isn't always ideal, and I expect our CEO and sales director to have offices at our facility.

My companies, Hunt Advantage Group LLC and Pizza Wholesale Company, have our main facility in Paris, Kentucky. It is a beautiful, modern office and distribution center. On a weekly basis, we ship everything (that the stores need for serving our pizza) to 28 satellite warehouses in 18 states. Overall, Hunt Brothers Pizza (of which my two businesses are a part), ships weekly to 54 satellite warehouses in 28 states. Working from their warehouses, our fantastic sales professionals deliver the needed pizza products to the stores in their area. The real action is in the field where the best ideas are generated. The Sales Director is in the field 80% of his time. The CEO is in the field at least 20% of his time. The field is where the rubber hits the road; it's where we visit our customers and also spend time with the men and women who are servicing those customers each week.

No matter how much management we have, the most important person in the company is the one who sees the customers each week. If that person is hired as the result of an intelligent choice made by the company, trained properly, treated with respect as a brother or sister, and paid fairly, there usually isn't a need for much management. The government of the United States is top-heavy. Most companies are top-heavy. The best operation is lean, with less management, where more money is given to the person who is eyeball to eyeball with the customers. That person truly represents the company!

– 26 –

Plan Your Work and Work Your Plan

How many times have we heard "Plan your work and work your plan" and attempted to do just that—even for a day or two? Again, discipline is needed to plan your work and work your plan.

What follows is the way I attempt to accomplish this objective. I've found it to be one of the best ways to do so. I write down my schedule for the coming day, numbering my priorities from 1 to 10 in order of importance. In the morning I work on the first one until it's finished, if possible, then move on to the next. Most likely, I will not get through all 10 that day, but that evening I will make a new list of priorities for the next day. The priorities may change positions based on their importance.

If I'm scheduled for a meeting, I plan in my schedule to be there on time. If I cannot be there on time, I phone ahead. To be late for an appointment without phoning shows a lack of integrity. Lateness for a scheduled appointment without phoning to explain "red flags" a person's integrity, reliability, and regard for others' time. If you see you'll be late, it's very important to phone beforehand and explain.

– 27 –

Persistence

Webster's says persistence is to go on resolutely or stubbornly in spite of difficulties. It's the desire to do a certain thing so much that virtually nothing can stop you.

Businessman, author, and philanthropist W. Clement Stone tells the story of selling newspapers on the street one morning as a young boy around 8 years of age. It was so cold and windy on that winter morning in Chicago that he stepped through the front door of an upscale restaurant just to get out of the wind for a minute. A man at one of the tables beckoned him to come over. The man bought a paper from him for a nickel and tipped him a dollar. Stone looked around the restaurant at all the people sitting at the tables and took ownership of that restaurant. He then went from table to table asking the customers to buy a paper. His sales were easier than they had ever been, and he sold a lot more papers that morning than he had ever sold in the same amount of time out on the street.

The owner saw him and told him he couldn't sell newspapers in his restaurant. The next day Stone went back into the restaurant and resumed selling papers, and again he was told to leave. The day after that he was back in the restaurant selling papers, and the owner saw him and was angry. He said to young Stone, "I told you not to come back. Now you get out of here, and don't come back." About that time a person at one of the tables yelled, "Harvey! Hey, Harvey! Let the boy sell papers in here. We like him, and we want to buy papers from him." Someone else said, "Yeah, Harvey, leave the kid alone." The restaurant customers told the owner to let Stone sell his papers to them because they appreciated his persistence and wanted to buy the newspapers from him. The owner relented. Stone had persisted, and because he did, he was successful.

Stone went on in life to become very financially successful. He built a billion-dollar insurance company and is known for the books he wrote and the millions of dollars he gave to help others. In Zig Ziglar's *Born to Win* series Stone is quoted as saying, "Definiteness of purpose is the starting point of achievement." That sums up persistence. A burning desire to do a certain thing until it's accomplished. And to quote movie actor Sylvester Stallone, "How hard can you get hit and keep moving forward?"

A salesman leaves his home or business in the morning, determined to give three presentations that day. Having given two presentations, it's now past 6 p.m., dinner is waiting, it's starting to get dark, and he wants to call it a day, but he has committed to giving three presentations. He persists and finds that third presentation audience, and that last presentation, as it so often does, results in his only sale for the day.

You must be persistent in pursuing your objective of staying physically, mentally, socially, and spiritually fit. Take a page from young Jesus. Luke 2:52 says, *"And Jesus grew in wisdom and stature, and in favor with God and men."* That's a four-legged chair. Persistence involves day-in and day-out exercise through stretching, biking, walking, running, or swimming. It involves reading and listening to the good stuff—the motivational and educational stuff—that will help you relate more effectively to people in your chosen profession. Reading the Word of God daily will help you grow spiritually. The four disciplines of the Luke passage—mental, physical, spiritual, and social—are all connected. It is so important to be committed to all four of these forms of fitness throughout your life.

> Nothing in the world can take the place of persistence. Talent will not; nothing is more common than unsuccessful people with talent. Genius will not; unrewarded genius is almost a proverb. Education will not; the world is full of educated derelicts. Persistence and determination alone are omnipotent.
>
> —Calvin Coolidge
> *30th president of the United States*

– 28 –

Leadership

We start out in life learning from others. Our parents are our first teachers and should be our best. There are things we can learn only from our parents and from our brothers and sisters. No one outside the home teaches us how to be good husbands or wives. No one outside the home teaches us how to be good parents. As we grow up, we listen as our parents and siblings make decisions that are true leadership decisions. I was fortunate to have two older brothers who were leaders, as well as a father and mother who were leaders. All through grade school and high school, my brothers and parents set a leadership pace. No matter what I did or where I went in our hometown, I was received with respect as a Hunt. My father and brothers had respect as leaders in the community. In our neighborhood there also were other leaders. While playing neighborhood football, basketball, and baseball—and even pole-vaulting into our homemade sandpit—I saw leadership not only in my brothers but in other neighborhood kids as well. You knew a guy was a leader when he suggested going fishing or doing something—and everyone jumped on the bandwagon. You couldn't help but notice how he spoke and acted in a way that drew everyone to his ideas. I remember the man who told ghost stories on his back porch. The parent who showed movies every Saturday night in his backyard was also a leader.

My parents put us older brothers into leadership roles early in life. We babysat the younger children and were given certain chores. Working in our father's restaurant, we were given the opportunity to make decisions that affected the lives of the older employees who worked beside us. We learned to respect these people, and we learned to ask them to do things rather than demand things of them. We gained their respect because we worked as hard as they did and could do the work as well as they could. We learned that if we wanted respect from others, we must show them respect. Of course, when our father died

> *We learned that if we wanted respect from others, we must show them respect.*

when I was 16, my brothers and I were thrust into even more leadership roles, especially at the restaurant.

My formal education began in a Catholic grade school. After attending a Catholic seminary for 2½ years, I finished my high school at Memorial, a Catholic school back in Evansville. The ocean and Tampa University in Florida held my attention for a couple of years until my family called me home to manage the Austin's restaurant. At age 21 I was drafted into the military and chose the Marine Corps. In all those settings I listened to and observed many leaders who helped shape my life. Through the years I discovered that the really good leaders knew where they were going and motivated others, who followed them because they bought into their vision. The successful leaders gave their followers the opportunity to achieve their potential by giving them responsibilities, whereby they could grow and become leaders themselves. Giving others the opportunity to lead was, they knew, the only way to grow beyond their own talents and efforts. Leaders thereby gain loyalty and respect from their people and exponential growth, beyond what their own time and abilities are capable of yielding. I discovered that truly great leaders are both humble and concerned about the people they lead. They take their leadership very seriously, knowing their decisions will impact the lives of those they lead. They understand they can't realize a vision by themselves, that they need other people—both leaders and followers. Leaders know that in order to replicate themselves, they must grow other leaders. They must invest time and energy in those individuals. As a king might put a ring on his son's finger to show his son's authority, leaders must give those they lead the ring of power, the authority to make decisions that will grow an enterprise.

Vince Lombardi, the legendary football coach, has been quoted as saying, "Leaders are made; they are not born. They are made by hard effort, which is the price that all of us must pay to achieve any goal that is worthwhile."

It was only when I made the decision to operate my business as though I were in a wheelchair that my company started on the path of exponential growth. When you are forced to be in a wheelchair, you can't lead the charge in battle. It isn't within your realm of possibility to travel in the field and grow a business area from a wheelchair. Again, you have to depend on your team to carry on your principles and do the physical labor if you want a company to grow. You have no choice but to depend on your team. This means you have to give the team direction, a vision for the future. You must lead the team with wisdom, motivating your people and guiding them toward your goals. Your goals must become the team's goals. You must motivate your people to take ownership of your vision. You must show true respect for your people and offer them a strong financial incentive for giving their best. Standing by your word at all times is essential. Showing you have faith in your team members and standing by their decisions also are highly important. Your people must be held accountable for their decisions and performance—and commended when they make the right decisions.

Bad decisions are made. This is not only acceptable, it's even to be celebrated. In my company, we would rather have someone who makes decisions than someone who is afraid to do so. There's a saying in chess that "a bad plan is better than no plan at all." There's a saying in business about decision makers: "If 50% of their decisions are right, they'll be successful." In life, no one can make all the right decisions all the time.

> *There's a saying in business about decision makers: "If 50% of their decisions are right, they'll be successful."*

During my life in business I've had people tell me things about team members that some might have considered serious enough to justify discharge. I had a choice. I could confront the person who was talked about or put the matter in the back of my mind and watch for signs concerning the matter. Most of the time if the person was doing a good job, I didn't discuss the matter with him but instead gave the matter time to surface on its own if it was indeed true. I gave the person the benefit of the doubt.

Gossip has no place in the leader's life. Talking negatively about another team member has no place in leadership. A leader discusses a team member problem with the person's manager and the company's HR person. A leader should never have to threaten his team members. If a leader ever gets to the point where he is threatening someone, he's only showing poor leadership. Long before it gets to that point, an employee should be asked to leave, assuming that claims of improper conduct have been substantiated. Showing anger has no place with a leader. Self-control should be a major goal of a leader. If an employee doesn't follow the principles or certain guidelines of the company, it may be that he doesn't understand them, and in that case they should be explained to him. Once the person indicates understanding, a leader should expect future compliance with those principles and guidelines. If such behavior again happens, only then is it time to wish the person a good future somewhere else.

I recommend doing this by sitting with the person and explaining to him (or her) why it's time to part company: "Joe, evidently this isn't the best position for you, since you aren't following our policies. We believe it best for you to resign and find some other work that will be more to your liking. You must realize we're asking you to resign, but if you decline, we'll have to let you go. It's your choice." Many people appreciate the opportunity to resign rather than being fired.

As a leader it's important that you help your team understand the *why*—the reasons *why* certain decisions are made. Make it a policy to explain the reasons for doing things a certain way. Be very clear so that the team truly understands the reasons; the team will then be much more likely to pull together with you to accomplish the mission.

There have been times in my life when serious decisions had to be made concerning people in my regional managers' areas. I would determine what I thought should be done before contacting the regional manager. When I would speak to him and explain the problem, I would ask him what *he* thought we should do. There have been times when his decision was different from what I had in mind. If he felt strongly that his way was best—and he had good reasons for his convictions—I would tell him to go ahead and handle the matter his way. If I disagreed with the way he proposed to resolve it, naturally I would explain my point of view and then ask his opinion.

Why did I do this as a leader? Shouldn't I have stood by my decision come hell or high water? Allowing my regional manager to go with his way of handling a situation produced pride within him and gave him the need to prove to me that his decision was the right one. It empowered him; he took ownership of the problem and the solution. Empowerment of the team and assignment of ownership are precisely what a leader wants. One of the worst things that can happen to a good employee is to have someone else's idea forced on him and be obligated to carry that idea forward. Let your people think and help you come up with the best ideas if you want wholehearted participation in an outcome.

To be a successful leader you must bring into your circle those people who have the expertise that you lack. Gifted men and women who can advise you and help you accomplish your goals. You need a strong team of leaders who work well together. They must share your vision and your ethics.

The General Sherman, a giant sequoia in California, stands over 200 feet tall and has a 70-foot circumference. It's more than 2,000 years old. You would think its roots must reach to China, but the fact is that sequoia trees have roots that reach just barely under the ground. You might ask how they can withstand strong winds with such shallow roots. Sequoias grow only in groves, and their roots intertwine with those of their neighbors under the surface of the earth. When strong winds come, they hold each other up. Alone, they would never stand up to the winds of California.

People are like the sequoias. When the high winds of adversity blow, strong team members can serve as reinforcement and encouragement, helping each other stand together and reaffirm their beliefs and commitments.

– 29 –

Early Struggles as a Salesman

Life is full of challenges, and meeting those challenges "head on" grows and develops you into the person you hope to be. The easy way out is to ignore the challenges, but by doing so you become afraid and can't grow.

After my eye-opening experience at age 11—when I sold apple pie to a man in my father's restaurant (see Chapter 8)—I became a believer in asking either/or questions instead of yes/no questions. During the next decade working at Austin's "Drive Up" Restaurant, I discovered that people usually don't think about what they want—and suggestions trigger their wants or needs. Whether we know it or not, as noted in Chapter 22, we all sell ourselves daily. We sell ourselves to our teachers, our employers, our parents, our in-laws, our children, our brothers and sisters. Actually to everyone we meet and

For sure, we sell ourselves daily in all areas of our life.

ultimately to our life partner.

I received Red Cross lifeguard training at the YMCA while attending college in Tampa, Florida. As mentioned in Chapter 8, I was then able to sell myself as a qualified lifeguard and acquired work as a lifeguard, even though I had no actual experience as such and had only the training. Because I sold myself to the employment office of my college, I worked for a canning factory while I was a student. I also managed to become a tour guide for the grand opening of a new brewery in Tampa. During my four years in the Marine Corps I sold myself to various employers (again, see Chapter 8) and also gained meritorious promotions while in the infantry and motor transport, as well as the S-4 Logistics office. For sure, we sell ourselves daily in all areas of our life.

About three months after being discharged (in early 1966) from the Marines, I started work with my brothers' company,

Wholesale Pizza Company out of Nashville, Tennessee, the name of which would later be Pepe's Pizza. Charlie, my younger brother, also was in the pizza business by this time. He was only 19 years old when he left college and started the first pizza route for Don's company in Evansville. Don says he had no idea about building his small pizza route in Nashville anywhere else. He was just making a living for his family when Charlie asked Don to get him started selling pizza in Evansville. Charlie built a very profitable business in Evansville, then Lonnie came on board and built in Memphis, Tennessee. When I came back from California and started in the business, Don's Wholesale Pizza Company was in Evansville, Memphis, Nashville, and Huntsville, Alabama. We give Charlie credit for showing us we could do this anywhere.

After training (which basically consisted of riding along with Don for a week), my first challenge in the spring of '66 was to put the company's pizza program in restaurants, bars, drive-in movie theaters, and pizza houses—anywhere pizza could be sold. This was cold-call selling. It meant walking into a store without the owner knowing I was coming and without the owner knowing anything about the product or the company. The last thing on the owner's mind when I walked in was pizza. So each morning I headed down the street, walked into the first place that I thought could sell pizza, and asked for the owner. If the owner was available, I introduced myself and said that I would like to bake him or her a pizza and explain our program. Sounds simple enough, right?

The problem was that at the age of 25 years I had no experience in cold-call selling. My prior experience in selling—with Success Motivation Institute out of Waco, Texas—was with scheduled appointments. There's a true fear factor that most of us have to get past to be successful in the art of cold-call selling. Getting past that fear factor was a true challenge for me, just as it is at first for most who attempt it. Some never get over the fear and never master this type of selling. I found all kinds of excuses for not going into stores to talk to people. Because of fear, I often drove past a store looking for one that seemed less threatening. I drove miles out of the way to call on prospects that were less fear-inducing before calling on those who were right near me.

There were times when I actually went back to my apartment, listened to records on selling, and went back out to call on stores, having gotten the courage to do so. When I was 25 years of age, there were only vinyl records; there wasn't all the modern technology we have today, which includes cassettes and CDs. I was listening to inspirational records every day and even turning them on while going to sleep at night. I needed anything and everything I could read or listen to in order to have the confidence to walk into a store, face a stranger, and expect to walk out with her money in my pocket. I finally got to the point where I would pull over and stop after driving by a store because of fear. I would make myself turn around, go back to that store, and face my fear. I remember telling others that whenever I did this turnaround, I almost always ended up selling the company's pizza program. By facing the fear, I overcame it.

Eventually there came a time when it was no longer much of a challenge to make a sale; it had become relatively easy to close a sale. I had climbed the mountain and overcome my fear. It took time and many calls for this to happen. It's the same with speaking in public. It *is* a challenge, and the way to overcome any challenge is to face it, take ownership of the situation, and gain confidence by practice. Action is the answer when there's indecision or fear. If we take the first step, the second step will come easier.

> *The way to overcome any challenge is to face it, take ownership of the situation, and gain confidence by practice.*

Staying right with God, our Creator, is vital for maintaining self-confidence and overcoming any challenges in life. In order to think straight and have wisdom and courage, I believe keeping ourselves spiritually in tune with God is essential. It's so very true that *we can do all things through Christ, who strengthens us,* as Paul puts it in Philippians 4:13—and that without Him we are nothing.

– 30 –

How to Make Good Decisions

Every day we have decisions to make, and it seems that decision making in life goes in cycles. Have you noticed that there are times in your life when things are calm with no real pressures, but then there are times when serious decisions must be made? Times when you are extra busy and times when you just glide through the day and have time to smell the roses? Life goes in cycles, and we must learn to appreciate whatever place in the cycle we're in at the time. It's the same with problems in our lives. We have the joyous births of our children and grandchildren, and we have the deaths of our loved ones. We must prepare our minds and spirits to accept these times and decide that life has ups and downs—and that it's up to us to ride the waves and stay on an even keel. This is a decision that each of us can make, and it's a wise one.

Worry is a by-product of making decisions, and unless we plan our decision making, worry becomes our master. Most worry isn't necessary and shouldn't be tolerated. In my life, most of the things I've worried about never ended up happening.

> *Worry is a by-product of making decisions, and unless we plan our decision making, worry becomes our master.*

Many years ago I experienced anxiety that turned out to be unnecessary and even cost me a speeding ticket. I left my motel in Pound, Virginia, at 6 a.m. to service my customers, knowing that I would get home around 9 p.m. if all went well. The weatherman on the radio said that a fierce snowstorm was on its way, so everyone should plan on getting off the roads as quickly as possible by day's end. The news of the snowstorm grabbed my attention, so I hit the panic button—and the accelerator—and tried to rush through the day. Pretty soon a police car, siren blaring, came up behind me, and sure enough

I received a ticket for speeding. I told the officer about the coming snowstorm and why I was in such a hurry to get home. He said, "Be careful so you *can* get home safely; the storm may miss us."

Here's the rest of the story: The snowstorm never happened. My anxiety was a waste of time. I should've surrendered the problem to God and gone on through the day resting in the knowledge that whatever happened happened. We live in a time when the news media are forecasting many negative things. Usually the news is much more negative than positive. It's important not to worry and to put your trust in the Word of God. Remember, most newscasters thrive on news that will stir up their listeners.

Your business decisions may affect many people; therefore, it's wise to call on others for their thoughts. While this means you'll get both good and bad advice, you must find out all the pros and cons of a course of action. Although you shouldn't be in a hurry to make decisions, there are times when you're up against the wall and decisions must be made. Many a military general has had to make a life-and-death decision quickly, and all that could be done was get as many facts together as possible and make the decision.

Get the facts, write down the advantages and disadvantages of each choice, and always make your decision on ethical grounds. Ask yourself, *What is the right decision according to God's principles?* and *What would Jesus do?* Decisions based on God's principles aren't always easy to make, but in the long run they stand firm.

There have been a few occasions when I made a decision and later received information that caused me to change it. In the opinion of some, changing a decision is a sign of weakness and poor leadership. It has been said that a strong leader never changes his decision, no matter what. But as I have grown older and wiser, I've realized that it makes a lot of sense to change a decision when new information calling for a change is brought forward. I would rather be humble and change a decision when I know it should be changed rather than "stick to my guns" at all costs. I'm reminded of the sad-but-true statement of all too many people: "My mind is made up; don't confuse me with facts."

I've learned from those experiences that it's very important to take the time to get information from all directions before you make a decision. If you take the time to get all the information, it will be much less likely that you will have to face changing your decision later. Taking time now can save a lot of grief later.

– 31 –

Healthy Living

February 2011

> As I sit here on the island of Tortola in the British Virgin Islands, looking across the sea at the islands of St. Thomas and St. John, I must say this is a paradise.

I am 71 years of age, going on 40, but I am aware that the body doesn't always agree with the brain on this matter. Somewhere around the age of 60 I noticed some change in the health of my knees that motivated me to stop running and start walking and riding a bike instead. Then, around the age of 68, pain in my knees and back caused me to have to do things in a way contrary to what I had taken for granted throughout my life. A herniated disc I developed had me limping and using a cane.

Having gone to chiropractors four or five times a week for almost a year, I discovered Bikram hot yoga. Participants in this type of yoga spend 90 minutes in a 105-degree room doing two sets of 26 stretches. Bikram Choudhury's teaching is that these stretches, which he has designed over a 50-year yoga career, will cure most any ailment and especially those of the back. After only six sessions I had no pain in my back.

I have been a very active person all my life. Early in my life I busied myself with football, basketball, baseball, some track events, tennis, keep-away, swimming, and wrestling with just my father and brothers. In college I was involved in crew racing (synchronized power rowing) and a lot of tennis. In the Marines, along with all the hiking, I became an avid runner, and I continued running until I was 60. I always read that people should stretch before and after running or even walking, but I seldom took the time. Now I know the importance of stretching. Though I was a serious runner, I question excessive running because of the danger it poses. The continual pounding of the lower body against hard surfaces during running can damage your knees. Many who were runners when they were young develop knee problems later in life and can't continue. You'll find that many older men and women who now run didn't when they were young.

At this time in my life I practice hot yoga at least three times a week, along with walking four days a week or riding a bike. Each morning I start the day with stretches and crunches, and I use a ROM (range of motion) exercise machine every day I'm home and not away on business or vacation.

> *All healthy foods should be enjoyed in moderation.*

There are many varieties of healthy food—and it would be a shame to limit ourselves to the unhealthy options. All healthy foods should be enjoyed in moderation. I believe that people today have a tendency to overeat, and most restaurants' and fast-food establishments' food portions are entirely too large. Most such portions could be shared by two people, and both parties would have plenty to eat. Cheryl and I would share our meals most of the time, and we found we were completely satisfied, plus it cut our meal bill in half. Sometimes the restaurant people would still give each of us a regular serving, possibly thinking we were concerned about the cost, not realizing it wasn't so much the cost as the fact that we didn't want to eat so much.

For the past three years my way of eating has been thus: My first meal of the day is a delicious smoothie that I will describe in Chapter 37. Throughout the day I try to eat a serving of protein as big as my fist and a serving of carbohydrate of similar size every three hours. Examples of what I eat during the day include tuna, fresh spinach, and a fruit. I'll also have one main meal a day, preferably late afternoon, around 4 p.m. For my main meal I eat pretty much what I want to eat, but I have only one serving.

Moderation is key. When we're young we take health for granted and eat it all and drink it all, but as we get older we learn that moderation is important. I do believe that God has given us so many things to enjoy—including miraculously formed bodies that are continually renewing themselves. But we must take in the proper food, the proper fuel, to maintain these wondrous machines. Our bodies also must move in order to stay lubricated and healthy. This means we must have a plan of action and work our plan. When I was in college I worked for a time in a gym helping others get in shape. For many reasons most of the people I helped didn't stick with their programs. Later I joined gyms myself, but I found going to the gym and then showering and changing clothes to be a hassle; it took too much time. I prefer to do my workout early in the morning at home. In my book the very best workout is to do easy crunches and stretches followed by walking, riding a bike, or swimming. When it's too cold outside to work out, use of a machine like a stationary bike or a treadmill is ideal.

[See also Chapter 37 for more thoughts on healthy living.]

– 32 –

How to Relate to the Opposite Sex

> Today I'm in a comfortable room at Natural Bridge State Resort Park in Kentucky. It is April 2011; the temperature is in the 70s. I stole away to write for a few days, and I'm enjoying hiking and appreciating the beauty of one of Kentucky's outstanding state parks. The food here is always well prepared and delicious.

I intentionally used a "grabber" of a title for this chapter. Do I have your attention?!

The opposite sex is a mystery to most of us. Now, since I'm a man, since I was married to a woman for 38 years, and since I have four beautiful daughters, all of whom are more than 21 years of age, I believe I have the right to voice my opinion.

But first, I think it would be appropriate for me to briefly recount my encounter and courtship with Cheryl Grotius, who was to become the love of my life.

At 29 years of age I had spent time in college and more than four years in the Marines, as well as traveled in many states building the pizza business, but I had not yet met a woman I loved and wanted to marry. My sister Mary Christine worked with Cheryl at a hospital in Evansville, Indiana. On an Easter weekend when all the family was home, Mary invited Cheryl to spend an evening with us—and she was just as sweet that weekend as she was the 38 years we were married. We dated for a year, but since I lived in Nashville and traveled, you might say we actually dated for a total of just three months. We married when I was 30 and she was 22.

Women are so precious, and they are a true gift from God for their children and for us men. Little girls are so special, and this doesn't change when they grow up. If girls are raised with love, they respond with love.

For the young man looking for the right young lady to marry someday, realizing the dream can seem impossible. What follows is my advice to you.

First and foremost, *surrender* your desire to God by telling Him what you want but also telling Him you put your desire in

His hands. From that point on *trust* that God will answer your prayer. Now each day and throughout the day, thank and *praise* God for His answer to your prayer. Use STP—*surrender, trust,* and *praise.*

Each day, as you're going through your work and life, keep your eyes open to the single ladies you see and meet. If you see one who is attractive to you, say a prayer and ask God whether you should go over and speak to her. You should know that many beautiful single women are lonely because men don't have the courage sometimes to ask them out. You may think that because the one you've noticed is so beautiful, she is surely dating someone and won't have time for you. Nothing is gained, however, if you don't ask, and nothing is lost if she isn't interested. Just walk over and say, "Hi there!"

If you have peace about approaching the young lady and God, through the Holy Spirit, guides you to do so, walk over and say hello. Look her in the eyes, introduce yourself, speak truthfully, and tell her you saw her and wanted to speak to her. Ask her name, and ask whether she would be interested in doing something together sometime. If she says maybe, ask for her phone number. If your conversation goes on for a while, you may be able to line up a dinner date on the spot.

As I think about my daughters and my wife in the position of the young lady, I realize that they would each want a sincere man, who looked into their eyes while talking to them, not at their body. They would appreciate a man who didn't talk about himself unless they asked questions. A man should listen closely to everything a young lady says and show interest in what she is saying. A major gripe that women have is that men don't listen and don't show respect for them.

One of the biggest weaknesses I see in men today is in their treatment of women. A man should never tell a woman to phone him sometime. A man should pick a lady up at her home, not meet her somewhere. If she lives with her parents, the man ideally should meet them for the first date so that they know with whom their daughter is going out. A man should let a lady walk ahead of him through the door he is holding open. A man should open the door of the car when she is getting in and out. In the restaurant—ideally a nice restaurant on the first date—a man should pull her chair out when she sits down and when she gets up.

When you're with a woman, give her all your attention. The very worst thing you can do is look at another woman while you are with your date. It may be a challenge not to do so, but it is a big mistake to do so. Your first date is the perfect time to learn all about the woman you are with. It isn't the time to talk about yourself. When she asks about you, answer her, then turn the questions back to her again.

Remember, the way to win a friend is to listen. People don't listen as they should. It's not difficult to develop a good conversation when you're truly interested in the other person. In relationships, more is accomplished by listening than by speaking. You'll find that friendships grow far more by listening and responding to what is said than by speaking.

> *Remember, the way to win a friend is to listen.*

Where do you go to school? What is your major? How do you think you will use it after college? Is there anyone else in your family working in that field? Do you have any brothers or sisters? What kind of goals do you have for your life? What do you like in a guy? What kind of work does your older brother do? Have you ever been in a 5K run? Would you like to go hiking sometime? Do you think your sister could go with us? Do you have a dog? Would you like to go to church with me this Sunday? Do you like fried chicken? Do you like spinach? Your questions should be fun questions—but don't ask them in rapid-fire fashion. Work them in naturally.

Sometime during the evening you must compliment your date for her beauty. Your compliment must be honest, from your heart. Maybe it is the way she speaks that you find beautiful. It may be that her eyes are beautiful, so tell her how beautiful they are. Is it her hair, her smile? Maybe her hands are beautiful to you. Women don't know how much we men treasure them and all of who they are!

I believe that women want men with sincerity and integrity, men who can deliver security. Too many men have neither discipline nor solid values, and women understandably lose faith in men. A man who doesn't show respect for a woman before marriage certainly won't do so after marriage. If you truly love a woman, you don't take advantage of her. You don't ask her to prove her love by doing something that she doesn't believe is right. If you do this, you aren't loving her, you're using her. If you truly love a woman, you want the very best for her.

– 33 –

Marriage: Woman and Man Become One

Not long ago I was at the end of a pier on the island of Curaçao, in a fine open-air restaurant awaiting a whole red snapper for dinner. The ocean waves were crashing on the beach directly in front of me, and as I looked at the waves and the sway of the ocean, I was reminded of women. The way women look to us men. A woman doesn't always know the power she has in just her natural movements and her natural femininity. The graceful movements of her hands, the slenderness of her ankles, the elegant lines of her neck, the sparkle in her eyes—the whole package. God was so good to give Adam his Eve and to give us men women to love and share our lives with.

> *She is the heart of the marriage and the heart of the family. She will be like a diamond that sparkles ever brighter if she is continually treated with respect and love.*

The woman is vital to the longevity of a marriage. She is the heart of the marriage and the heart of the family. She will be like a diamond that sparkles ever brighter if she is continually treated with respect and love. But if she isn't respected and loved, she could turn into a dark, black piece of coal.

"A happy marriage is one that makes a woman more beautiful and improves a man's disposition," wrote my mother on a piece of paper I found in her Bible. Marriage is a two-way street; the man and the woman must love and respect each other for each to mature in the marriage. The Bible clearly states that the two will become one (Genesis 2:24). Ideally the man and woman will love each other unconditionally, share in all decision making, and sacrifice their personal desires for the good of one another.

My wife, Cheryl, and I were married for 38 years and together raised eight wonderful children. Speaking from experience, I humbly offer some advice:

- Each day thank God for giving you your partner for life.
- Every day tell and show your spouse, by your words and your actions, that you love him or her.
- Never go to sleep without resolving a disagreement with your spouse.
- Always kiss and hug your spouse before you leave the home and when you return.
- Husbands, at least one evening a week take your wife out on a date, and go someplace where you can sit and really listen to her and give her your full attention.
- Share your ideas and dreams, and show your appreciation for your spouse.
- Once a year, or more often if possible, get away together, just the two of you. It may be a hotel in the next town or even in your own town. It may be a retreat center 100 miles away. Steal away for a weekend. Husbands, surprise your wife at times with an unplanned getaway.

- Listen to your partner; really listen. Stop whatever you're doing and give him or her your full attention; listen so that you will understand. Men, this is very important to women. Respond to their ideas in an affirming manner.
- Never, never, never look at other women or men when you're out with your spouse. All your attention should be on your lifetime partner.
- Husbands, take your family on yearly vacations, during which you give your full attention to your wife and children. Don't take work along.
- Pray together—because the family that prays together stays together.

Allow me to elaborate on this last point.

When I started my business I had very little money but lots of confidence and enthusiasm, and Cheryl and I prayed together daily. We did so throughout our marriage. Each day, before I went out to sell, we held hands or just hugged and said, "Jesus, lead us to someone who wants our product even more than we want to sell it." We also prayed that I would have the opportunity to say the name of Jesus to someone that day.

As a family we prayed each day before meals and before the children went to bed. We just gathered together in the living room and prayed together. Throughout the day we prayed as different situations came up. With eight children in the house, belongings frequently got lost. They might have been shoes, other pieces of clothing, or workbooks. Everyone would look and get flustered until, finally, someone would say, "Let's say a prayer." Cheryl and I would ask Jesus to help our family find the lost item so that our children could see that He answers prayer. After the prayer Cheryl or I would say, "OK, go find that shoe." Every time we prayed one of the children found the lost item. Many times it was found immediately after the prayer.

Cheryl and I prayed together in bed at night. We thanked God for our children, our parents, our brothers and sisters, our business, and all the people who worked with the company. We prayed for the safety of our people in the field who drove so many miles each day. We prayed for wisdom in running the business and raising our children. We prayed that our children would find the partner for life whom God wanted for them.

Whenever Cheryl heard an ambulance or saw an accident, she would make the sign of the cross in that direction. Like me, she had grown up in a Catholic home.

My father showed us children by what he did and said that he loved our mother. Dad hugged and kissed Mom in front of us for no apparent reason. He always got up and pulled her chair out for her at the table at home and at restaurants. He kissed and hugged his wife and us when he left for work. He taught my brothers and me to open the car door for a lady, because he did it himself for his wife. I believe that these courtesies have been passed on to my children; they're things that further bond a family together.

– 34 –

Money and Marriage

It is important that a family be wise in its spending and saving. The spouse who wants the responsibility or is more capable of taking it should handle the finances. In a family with at least one or two good jobs, there shouldn't be financial problems if that family adheres to a budget.

Here's a simple system of budgeting that I use for my personal finances: If my pay period is one week long, I divide my monthly bill amounts by four. Each week, when I'm paid, I write the weekly budget amount for each monthly bill in my checkbook with an asterisk next to it, meaning that it has been put aside for the monthly bill. As an example, the monthly payment for a house may be $1,500. That would mean that $375 must be held back each week of the month. As far as I'm concerned, the $375 is no longer in the account. Then, when the monthly house payment is due, I just write the check and check off the budget figures that were listed each week.

I do the same with my credit card. I like the free flying miles Southwest Airlines provides, so most of the time I use a Southwest Visa credit card rather than cash. I use it as though it were a debit card in that I write the amount charged in my checkbook and deduct it from my checking account balance as though it were spent. I write *Deb* where the check number would normally go. When I receive my credit card statement, I just write the check. That way I never pay any interest.

Early in our marriage Cheryl and I decided to have just one credit card and not to use any department store cards. We both had use of the credit card, and I handled the checkbook. She had no problem with this. When a purchase requiring discussion needed to be made, Cheryl and I usually were able to agree on an amount that could be spent, an approach that kept us on the same page financially most of the time.

Cheryl didn't work outside the home, which was her choice. I believe that Cheryl not working outside the home was a major reason why we had a good family life experience. If she had wanted to work outside the home, I would have been with her 100% in her decision. However, I believe that if the husband is able to support the family financially, the wife can even more fully be what she already is: the true heart of the family. She is the glue that holds the family together. She is with the babies as they grow into children who are old enough to go to school. She's there when the children get home from school. When family members return home each day, she has dinner ready, that one meal the family can have together. In this way she usually can be available for the children and her husband.

I once learned a principle from something I read, and at some time in my life I made the wise decision to follow it. Once a year, when I change daily planners, I write the principle in the front of the new planner so that I can be reminded of it.

> ***This is wisdom:***
>
> If I have an idea for an investment or have a serious business decision to make, before I go through with it I must explain it to my wife. If I can explain it to her in such a way that she understands it and agrees with it, then I go forward with it. If I explain it to her and she

> cannot understand it or does not agree with it, I don't do it.

Many times in our marriage Cheryl had the wisdom that closed the door, or opened the door, on a decision regarding the growth of our business. You must understand that Cheryl was not working in our business, but God gives spouses tremendous intuition and wisdom, and we should respect and love them enough to bring them in on our major decisions. Marriage is a partnership with each other and with God.

Poor handling of finances can hurt a marriage. Happiness doesn't come from money but from our attitudes. Some of the happiest people may well be those of the Cofán tribe living in Zábalo in the Amazon Rainforest. Their homes are thatched, grass-domed huts with dirt floors, which blend into the forest as naturally as the trees. My understanding is that the Cofán live a simple but contented life, with almost none of the material things we take for granted. Their lifestyle is very different from ours—with our electrical appliances, cell phones, cable television, flushing toilets, clean water, and vehicles that start at the turn of a key.

All of these expensive conveniences make it important to have a sizable income—an income that requires time away from home. A woman may say to her husband, who is away from home too much building a business, that she would rather have him home than have all the conveniences. She may even say that she would be happy living in a shack if it meant he would be home more with the family.

This woman sincerely feels in her heart that she could be happy living with much less in order to have the family together more, but the truth is that just about all of us, husbands and wives alike, have become too accustomed to having material things. What the woman really means is that she wants her husband home a lot more *and* the material things. There has to be a middle ground, a trust and a faith that God will provide for our needs (though not necessarily all of our wants). We don't have to run so much and be so busy. Men, ask God for wisdom and for more time with your family. Ask God's angels to guide you toward a life that will allow you to both enjoy your family *and* provide for the family's needs. Listen to your wife, and adjust your life to give more time to your family, and you'll discover that your finances may even improve.

While on the subject of finances, there are people who believe that because they can't make their mortgage payments as a result of the recent economic downturn, the government should bail them out of their mortgages. I don't share this belief; I believe that mortgage holders need to take responsibility for their debts, come what may. We can agree, however, that there are reasons to give help in some cases. My purpose is not to judge people but to bring wisdom and discipline to financial decision making.

We must discipline ourselves to save, share, and buy—all with wisdom. When our first daughter, Yvette, started college, I borrowed money through her college's tuition finance system at a lower rate than that of other lenders—and with a 10-year repayment plan. But one day I read in the Bible that we should not borrow, because one day our lenders could come and take our beds from under us. After thinking about this and praying, I made a decision never to borrow again for our children's education. All eight of our children eventually attended college,

... Use money wisely, invest conservatively, and always share with those in need ...

and I never again borrowed for them to do so. We must use money wisely, invest conservatively, and always share with those in need as God lays awareness of need on our heart. When we give to help others and we do so from our heart, we are blessed even if sometimes the help is used wrongly by the recipients.

I have been asked many times by churches and other charitable groups to pledge a certain amount monthly, quarterly, or yearly. I don't believe in this. I do send money quarterly to some organizations and have done so for years, but I have never pledged to continue doing so, even for one further quarter. I may be led to discontinue, or I may find myself unable to continue. I refrain from making pledges, knowing that things may come up that could prevent me from honoring them.

To me, swearing and pledging are two peas in a pod. Jesus tells us not to swear to anything (Matthew 5:33–37). The Bible also shows that pledging can be a serious mistake. You may know the story in Acts 5 of Ananias and his wife, Sapphira, who pledged to give all the money they received for the property they were going to sell to further the work of the apostles. They didn't honor their pledge; they lied about the amount they received for the property and decided not to give the full amount. They hadn't been obligated to make a pledge, yet they did make one, but then they didn't honor it. Their failure to follow through cost them their lives. In my opinion, it's better to give as God leads; don't pledge anything to anyone.

Another goal to aim for is to be debt-free! It is possible—in a much shorter time than most would imagine. When you're debt-free, life looks different; you are the master of your life. Instead of paying interest, you're investing. Your confidence is improved. Men, your wife is happy, as security is so important to her.

The book *Debt-FREE & Prosperous Living* by John M. Cummuta is one of the very best guides to financial freedom that I've come across. This book contains the best teaching on how to become debt-free and what to do when you are free of debt. Cummuta's method has helped thousands, including me, accomplish the goal of freedom from debt. Paying off your mortgage in seven years instead of 30 and saving your family more than $100,000 in the process is just one example of freedom. Avoiding interest on your car payments and credit cards are other examples. Using that money instead to invest is exhilarating, and it is true freedom.

– 35 –

Raising Children

Certainly I'm no expert on child rearing, but Cheryl and I did raise eight intelligent, wise, healthy, mature, dependable, and financially responsible children.

As I've noted earlier, the woman, the mother, is the heart of the family. When the mother works outside the home and someone other than she cares most of the day for her young child, she isn't there for the child, and her love is missing from the child's life throughout the day. Cheryl breast-fed all our children, and breast-feeding makes a big difference in children's development. It's the daily caring, holding, kissing, hugging, and loving that make such a difference.

In his *Born to Win* series, Zig Ziglar talks about a study that compared the number of infant fatalities in a Mexican hospital with the number of such fatalities in a respected and very sanitary hospital in New York. The Mexican hospital had been discovered to have considerably fewer baby deaths than the New York hospital. The study found that while the New York nurses fed the babies, changed them, and put them back into their cribs, the Mexican nurses sat with the babies, held them, kissed them, and loved and hugged them day and night. This accounted for the difference. Because of all the loving and hugging, there were fewer infant deaths.

We enjoyed our children and loved them. As stated previously, Cheryl never worked outside the home. We usually ate dinner together, and the family knew what time dinner was served. Our meals were invariably delicious, and mealtime was filled with laughter and stories and sometimes lots of noise.

Cheryl was a wonderful storyteller, and I think storytelling is important in a family. Music was also a major part of our family life. Cheryl had a beautiful singing voice and sang spontaneously throughout the day. She whistled beautifully as well. Very early in our marriage I surprised Cheryl with a baby grand piano because I knew she wanted one—and I enjoyed her singing and piano playing. She also taught herself to play the guitar. Because of the support for music in our family, all of our children developed wonderful singing voices, and most can play the piano by ear. Yvette, our first child, majored in voice at the University of Kentucky. Like her mother, she has a beautiful singing voice.

When it comes to raising children, I believe that loving them unconditionally, just as Jesus loves us, is the best gift we can give them. There is, however, such a thing as tough love. Believe me, there are times when children need a good spanking, but it's very important to explain to them the reason for the spanking and then express our deep and abiding love for them. Children often try to take advantage of their parents—and play one off against the other if they can. They catch on fast. As babies, they

When it comes to raising children, I believe that loving them unconditionally, just as Jesus loves us, is the best gift we can give them.

cry until their parents pick them up or until they go to sleep. Cheryl and I learned rather quickly that babies want to be picked up and would like to sleep with their parents. It wasn't easy at first, but we learned we had to shut the door and let the children cry until they fell asleep. It didn't take long for our infants to understand that crying didn't get them their way.

When I told one of my children something, I wanted to say it just once. Rather than yell at the child or say it again, I would get a rolled-up newspaper and walk over and "bop" him or her lightly with it. In this way the children caught on pretty quickly that I was going to say something only once, and they'd better pay attention.

When the children were told to do something, I expected it to be done and done correctly. There's a right way and a wrong way to do most things. We once had a handyman on whom we called at times to fix small things in our hundred-year-old home. He usually left us a mess to clean up after he did his work and left the house. Wood shavings and whatever else he dropped would be on the floor. We attempted to train our children to complete a job's whole process and do the job the very best they could the first time—if they were going to do a job at all. I'm reminded of the poem (author unknown) I learned as a child; it still applies today.

> If a job is once begun
> Never leave until it's done
> Be the labor great or small
> Do it well or not at all.

What follows is another poem containing some principles that we attempted to teach our children. This author also is unknown. We had it on the bathroom wall for our children to see daily. It's called "Golden Rules for Living."

> If you open it, close it.
> If you turn it on, turn it off.
> If you unlock it, lock it up.
> If you break it, admit it.
> If you can't fix it, call in someone who can.
> If you borrow it, return it.
> If you value it, take care of it.
> If you make a mess, clean it up.
> If you move it, put it back.
> If it belongs to someone else and you want to use it,
> get permission.
> If you don't know how to operate it, leave it alone.
> If it's none of your business, don't ask questions.
> If it isn't broken, don't fix it.

If it will brighten someone's day, say it.
If it will tarnish someone's reputation, keep it
to yourself.

– 36 –

Thanksgiving Is a Time for Thanks

I sent this to all the team members of our pizza company in November 2007, the last Thanksgiving that Cheryl was with us.

As I contemplate Thanksgiving at this time of my life and write to you my thoughts, I have to go back to my younger years, to the years before my father died. I was 16 when my father died. My oldest brother was only 21, and the youngest of our family was only 1 year of age.

My years growing up were good years, happy days. We had time to daydream; to trade comic books; play marbles; play football, baseball, basketball; play hide and seek; pole vault; high jump; and tell ghost stories until late at night. We were busy and active.

My family of seven brothers and sisters was more fun than a barrel of monkeys. Our mother and father were good parents.

They knew right from wrong, and we learned the difference pretty quickly. Our meals together every evening were the highlight of the day. Wonderful food prepared to perfection and shared with enthusiasm. Platters of skillet-fried chicken, fried pork chops, and salmon patties on Friday. Real mashed potatoes with gravy and pork roast. You had to move fast if you wanted the last piece. Lip-smacking good!

At our table my father ruled the roost. He was a good man and a lot of fun, but he said what he meant and meant what he said. When he suggested something to us boys, we knew he meant for us to do it, even though he made it seem like a suggestion. He was a teacher and a father who had our respect. He showed us that he loved our mother, and this strengthened our love for him.

Our Thanksgiving meals and days were very special. Since Dad had a restaurant he worked seven days a week, but Thanksgiving Day was spent with the family. He would take us boys to the river, and we would shoot bottles that we threw in the river using Dad's .22 rifle. That time with our father was very special.

> *We have so much to be thankful for, no matter what our circumstances.*

On arriving back home, the smell in the house was electrifying. The aroma of turkey with all the goodies was almost too much to bear. There weren't any fast-food restaurants in those days, so we were hungry when we sat down to eat with the family.

Always we prayed before our meals and then dived in to this magnificent feast … turkey, mashed potatoes and gravy, green beans, cranberry sauce, dressing, two or three other sides and desserts, apple pie, pecan pie, pumpkin pie, and blackberry cobbler with ice cream.

As I think back, I don't remember that our family took the time to tell each other the many things we were thankful for. If we didn't do this, I believe we missed a wonderful opportunity to show our love for each other and to our Father in heaven. We have so much to be thankful for, no matter what our circumstances. When I was 12 years old, I found this on a cardboard plaque in a store and bought it. I still have it in my library: “I felt bad because I had no shoes until I saw a man who had no feet.”

Take the time this Thanksgiving to thank our Lord and each other for all the wonderful blessings we are given. My family wants to thank each of you for being who you are and for what you do daily. You truly are a blessing to those you service inside and outside the company.

Love,

Cheryl, Jim Hunt, and Family

11/15/07

– 37 –

How to Start Your Day

What I share below is the way I start each day, but I'm sure there are many other ways that also are excellent.

Having lived these 73 years I've discovered that my spiritual and physical lives are closely intertwined. First thing in the morning I thank Jesus for letting me see another day. We're more likely to be thankful in this way as we get older. When we're young we tend to take our health for granted. Our bodies, with thousands of "moving parts," are truly miracles of God's creation, and it's amazing to me that they work as well as they do as long as they do. Psalm 139:13–14 expresses it beautifully:

> *For you created my inmost being; you knit me together in my mother's womb. I praise you because I am fearfully and wonderfully made …*

After thanking Jesus for another day, I thank Him for giving me Cheryl for those 38 years. I thank Jesus for each of my children, their wonderful spouses, and their children. I thank Jesus for each of my brothers and sisters and their spouses. I thank Jesus for all of Cheryl's family. I thank Jesus for our business and for all the people who make up our business family.

Next, I do my daily reading of the Bible. My other daily reading is from Man in the Mirror, an organization founded by Patrick Morley to help men be the men God intended them to be.

After showering and shaving, I take my morning supplements with a glass or two of water. Sometimes I also have the juice from half a fresh-squeezed lemon mixed with warm water.

Then it's time for some nourishment, and just about every day I have a tall glass of my own smoothie concoction. This starts with 8 ounces of coconut water, fruit juice, or carrot juice poured into a blender. After adding four ice cubes, I toss in such ingredients as blueberries, blackberries, raspberries, strawberries, half a banana, a teaspoon of ground flaxseed, three teaspoons of lecithin, a scoop of chocolate-flavored Juice Plus, a teaspoon of protein powder, a half teaspoon of brewer's yeast, and a teaspoon of Blackstrap molasses—and mix the concoction in the blender. Believe it or not, it's delicious!

After this I'm ready to get some exercise. In my basement I have the equipment to become a bodybuilder, but my only intent is to stay limber and to remain healthy until the day I give up my spirit.

The first thing I do is put on a motivational CD, one containing a spiritual teaching or just some good music. Exercise time is a great opportunity to put good stuff into my mind for the day—so that the same good stuff will come out in various ways the rest of the day.

I have an exercise regimen that I follow seven days a week. It features stretching and stomach crunches. I believe the gut has to be kept in good condition because it is the core of the body. I use my ROM machine daily to work my upper and lower body. I jump on a miniature trampoline for a short time. I do

> *Throughout the day I praise God for my life and my health and everything else I can think of ...*

a stretching routine that is a back saver. At the end of my morning workout, I lie on my stomach and then on my back on a curved, half-moon table. This orientation puts my head lower than my heart; it's important to enhance blood flow to the brain.

I'm also into my third year of Bikram hot yoga (which, as noted earlier in Chapter 31, is different from other yoga stretching exercises). My goal is to practice yoga three to four days a week, then walk or ride a bike on the other days.

Throughout the day I praise God for my life and my health and everything else I can think of to be thankful for. I can't overemphasize the importance of thanking God all through the day for the many blessings that make up and fulfill our lives.

[See also Chapter 31 for more thoughts on a healthy lifestyle.]

– 38 –

How to End Your Day

The late Norman Vincent Peale, best known as author of *The Power of Positive Thinking*, recommended reading something joyful or spiritual before going to sleep so that we can dream of happy things. Peale predicted in one of his books that he would live a long life because he believed he would. He did indeed live a long life with a sound mind. Cheryl and I once attended the America's Awards ceremony in Washington, D.C., at the Kennedy Center and had the privilege of talking with Peale and his wife, Ruth—and give him a hug. He was 93 years of age at the time. He lived to be 94.

If you have any problems or decisions to make, I do believe you can get answers by surrendering them to God before going to sleep. It's true that God cares about your everyday concerns; all you must do is ask and He will meet your needs (see Matthew 6:25–34). I believe that after turning your concerns over to God before going to sleep, you may wake up with the answers. The subconscious mind—through dreams and otherwise—works on problems throughout the night. Your subconscious mind never sleeps, but while *you* sleep it searches for solutions.

Have you ever awakened at night and been unable to get back to sleep? When that happens to me, I find that if I just start thanking God for everything I can think of, I soon fall back to sleep. Sometimes when I wake up during the night, I feel the need to pray for someone, and I take that time to do so.

There have been a few times in my life when I have awakened at night in a cold sweat with much anxiety over a major decision I had to make. Whenever this happened I knew I had to surrender the decision to God and hold off making any move on the matter. Immediately I would give it to God and go back to sleep. There have been times when I have lain in bed working on a problem in my mind instead of sleeping. In order to stop this so that I could get my proper rest, I would turn the problem over to God and ask Him to provide a solution by morning.

Many times in my life I've worked late, knowing that I would have to get up early the next day with only four or five hours of sleep, so I would say this prayer: "Father, I ask that when I awake in the morning, I would feel like I have had 15 hours of sleep." Every time I've said this prayer, I've awakened several times during the night and checked the clock, thinking I had overslept. I would always wake up in the morning feeling like I had more than enough sleep.

Saying the prayer of Jabez, found in 1 Chronicles 4:10, is another wonderful way to start and end your day. Say to the Lord, *"Father, enlarge my territory for your glory. Let no evil come to me, and let me cause no pain."*

– 39 –

How to Face the Death of a Loved One

If you live long enough, you will witness people close to you pass on from this earth. Some will die peacefully, some because of old age, some because of medical problems, some in accidents. Dying, in my view, isn't something to be anxious about. Unless the Second Coming of Jesus occurs in our lifetime, our deaths are a given. Death is inevitable for all of us, and as I get older, having read about dying and seen others die, I don't believe it will be so bad. When it happens, I will be ready for it.

I remember the story of a young girl about the age of 13 who told her mother that she was afraid of marriage. The mother wisely responded that the child need not worry about it, that when the time came to be married she would be ready and would have no fear.

As you may already know, worry about something is generally much worse than the thing itself. Over the years I have seen my wife, my parents, one of my grandparents, my father-in-law, aunts, uncles, a nephew, good friends, and acquaintances die. It is the nature of life, the nature of humanity, to live for a time and then pass on.

Losing Cheryl in 2008 was a real blow to all of us. She was so vibrant and such a joy to be around. I had countless wonderful moments and memories with my dear wife. We were friends, lovers, and parents to our eight children. When I asked her, Cheryl would advise me regarding my business; she had so much wisdom. Our life together was good and wholesome—and I'm sure our marriage was put in place by God.

Her cancer had progressed over a two-year period, so when her time came we were prepared and believed it was best for her. The last thing she did as Zachary, our youngest child, was talking to her was shed a tear, and then she left us. Cheryl's funeral was a celebration of her new life promised by the

Word of God. She is still with us in spirit, and we believe we will see her again.

My father in his wisdom left his family the following words that are dear to my heart. He wrote:

> To each of my family.
> By night or by day,
> When loved ones are
> Thousands of miles away.
> If you remain pure, honest, and true,
> Take heart and don't be blue.
> We will sit down together again
> And talk just like we used to do
> In our new home in heaven
> Where we shall be forever happy
> And forever together.
> Love, Daddy

John 5:24 reads this way: *"I tell you the truth, whoever hears my word and believes him who sent me has eternal life and will not be condemned; he has crossed over from death to life."*

The death of a follower of Jesus is a time to *celebrate* entrance into heaven for eternity. If you believe in this entry into heaven, you are fortunate to be able to look death straight in the eye and surrender your loved one's spirit to God. You will

When I am gone, do not be sad for me;
But rather rejoice that my time has come,
And the second part of my journey has begun.

miss the person, and because of your love for one so close, a hole that can never be filled will certainly remain. There is sadness over the loss that will be with you for years, but you will go on living, and the sadness will fade after a while, and in its place will reside good memories that will not fade. There will be times when memories of something special that was part of your relationship will come to you in a flash. This may cause a tear or even a laugh, but it's OK because you know that you will meet again.

This is a note I want to leave to my children and grandchildren. I am 73 years of age at this point of my life. I have no intention of passing on soon, but who knows when that time will be. Naturally as one gets older there's a growing likelihood of the time being near, but many don't even see the age of 73. How many more years I still have on this earth is in the hands of God.

Dearest ones,
When I am gone, do not be sad for me;
But rather rejoice that my time has come,
And the second part of my journey has begun.

Thank you for the love you shared
And for the happiness you gave me;
Because of you, I am who I am,
And I thank you for that.

Sincerely I ask for no tears of sadness,
Yet tears of happiness I would beg;
Our lives are short and our purpose is clear:
Jesus is Lord of our lives for all eternity.

No flowers on the grave of my flesh,
Nor expensive stones to decorate it;
Rather give the money to help others
As God leads you each day.

Love,
Dad, Papa

– 40 –

Things I Would Do Differently if I Could Live My Life Over

At this writing there is nothing—other than the sins I've committed—that I would do differently if I had my life to live over. I believe God has had His hand on me throughout my life, through the great times and perhaps especially through the tough times. I have been clay in the hands of the Master.

God bless each of you in everything you say, everything you do, and everyone you touch.

About the Author

Jim Hunt is Co-Founder of Hunt Brothers Pizza with his three brothers: Don, Lonnie, and Charlie. HBP services more than 6,500 stores each week with all the products needed to serve the pizza. Included in the outstanding HBP team are many children, nephews, and nieces. This is a company that operates like a family yet maintains the precision of a fine-tuned business. Jim also is Founder and Chairman of Hunt Advantage Group and Pizza Wholesale of Lexington, Kentucky.

Jim was born August 5, 1939, in Evansville, Indiana, the third of four brothers. There followed three sisters: Elizabeth Ann (Meng), Theresa Agnes (Virga), and Mary Christine (DeWitz).

Jim's parents, James Austin Hunt and Matilda Barbara Stocker Hunt, were Roman Catholic. Jim had a Catholic education through high school. After his father died in late

1955 when Jim was 16, he and his brothers had to support the younger children and their mother. They took on the responsibility of running Austin's "Drive Up" Restaurant on Highway 41 in Evansville.

Jim attended Tampa University in Florida, then spent four years and three months in the U.S. Marine Corps just prior to the escalation of the Vietnam War. In 1966 he left California and returned to the Midwest to join his brothers in the pizza business. Over the ensuing years Jim made his home in Nashville, Tennessee; Gatlinburg, Tennessee; Paris, Kentucky; and Lexington, Kentucky.

Jim Hunt and Cheryl Grotius married in 1969; they had eight children: Yvette (Andrejczak), Erin (Ferguson), Frank, Todd, Rachel, Adam, Alexis (Peak), and Zachary. Jim and Cheryl had been married 38 years until her death in 2008. The past 18 years Jim has made his home in Lexington.

In his mid-30s, Jim had a spiritual awakening, which changed his life and that of his family. He says he titled this book *From Dawn to Dusk* as a way of describing life's journey from birth to old age. Now in his 70s, he wanted to share his